THE ISLE OF
FIRE MURDER

THE
ISLE OF FIRE
MURDER

Barbara Yager Witten

Walker and Company
New York

First published in the United States of America in 1987 by the Walker
Publishing Company, Inc.

Published simultaneously in Canada by John Wiley & Sons
Canada, Limited, Rexdale, Ontario.

Library of Congress Cataloging-in-Publication Data

Witten, Barbara Yager.
  The Isle of Fire murder.

  I. Title.
PS3573.I918I8   1987   813'.54   86-32510

ISBN: 0-8027-5677-8

Printed in the United States of America

10 9 8 7 6 5 4 3 2 1

I
Friday, July 1

1

AFTER IT WAS all over, after the last policeman left our tiny Fire Island community, I assigned a beginning. I'm the kind of woman who needs to assign one—in order to make sense out of something as senseless and unacceptable as murder. Sitting on the deck of my house high above the beach and the ocean, watching the sunset stain the sand pink and the waves purple, I settled on Friday afternoon at the ferry teminal on the mainland. Arbitrarily, of course, for I could have made a case for the morning three weeks earlier that June Milgrim opened her house for the summer, and Scotty Banks moved into her guest room. Or the night, two months before, that Caroline Mortimer's father died in his sleep in Fayetteville, Arkansas, and left her, among other things, his army gun. But I need to see a beginning firsthand, if I can, and I was there when we boarded the ferry, right in the middle of it when we crossed the bay and when we docked at Sharon's Landing. I was there, knowing in my bones that trouble was on the way.

It was a dry, cloudless afternoon, promising clear weather for the three-day Fourth-of-July weekend—though the promise would be broken. I was standing on the walk that led to one of the ticket windows, waiting (to pick up ferry schedules) behind a dark-haired young woman with a child in a stroller and a stocky, rough-looking man holding a big, restless German shepherd on a tight leash. The line had stalled. My old dog, Mops, peering through the mists of his cataracts at the sneakered feet collecting around us, pressed his rump against my ankles and whined for me to rescue him. I put down two-thirds of my bundles—a canvas tote and a shopping bag full of groceries—and as I picked up the dog, the dark-haired woman turned around and stared at me. Her empty gaze traveled from the undulating paper bag in my right hand, to the four pounds of elderly poodle pressed against my left shoulder.

"Where did you get that?" Her voice was low and flat.

I grinned at her. "The bag of lobsters or the dog?"

"That bunch of tickets." Stony-faced, she nodded at the green packet I was holding against the dog's dirty-white fur.

"In the ferry company office. I had to buy it there instead of here at the ticket window because I paid for it by check."

"What does it save you?"

"Over a dollar a ticket. Only you have to buy forty tickets in order to get the discount."

She shook her head. "We don't need forty. We're only renting for a couple more weeks. In a poky little place called Sharon's Landing. Nobody's ever heard of it."

"I have," I said dryly. "I have a house there."

"Dullsville, isn't it?" she offered, calmly trampling on my feelings. "Why don't you have a bar in the place?" she demanded. "Or a burger joint? Or a disco? Anyone who wants a little excitement has to be a goddamn athlete and hike through the sand for half an hour to get to Ocean Beach!"

"Not after today," I hurried to explain, hating myself for it. "It's high season now, and the lateral ferry's running. It'll take you from Sharon's Landing to Ocean Beach in five minutes. Or all the way up to Cherry Grove," I added, trampling on *her* feelings, "if ogling gays is your idea of excitement."

Why did she come to Sharon's Landing in the first

4

place, I wondered. Not for the sunshine; her skin was the color of a croupier's. And not for running around on our tennis courts, either. Her tight knit slacks outlined lumps of flab on her hip joints; she was as sedentary as a hen. If she'd wanted to spend her nights on a bar stool, why hadn't she rented somewhere else on Fire Island—Ocean Bay Park, or Kismet, or Ocean Beach itself?

"Whose house are you renting?"

She shrugged. "It's blue, on a corner across from the tennis-court gate. The owner writes for some magazine."

"He edits one," I corrected. "You're in Dan Ballou's house. Ballou. Like the color." Pushing myself, I managed to give her a neighborly smile. "I'm Lily Lambert. I own the yellow house up at the oceanfront."

She hesitated a moment. "I'm Dorothy Hayes. That's my husband, Carl."

The rough-looking man turned and faced me, pulling the German shepherd with him. The dog bared his teeth and growled at Mops.

Dorothy said, "This lady has a house in Sharon's Landing."

Carl Hayes looked me over as if I were a piece of unfamiliar merchandise. "Yeah," he grunted, blinking small mean eyes at my long, thick pewter-gray hair and my long, thin body, honed by weekly workouts in a gym and a thousand tennis games. Women in their very late forties, his look implied, should lose their teeth, run to fat, and henna their hair. The smile nudging the corners of my mouth died abruptly. He was studying the antique Navajo conches on the leather belt that held up my jeans, calculating their worth, his eyes hard as beach glass.

"Yeah," he muttered and dismissed me. With a tug on the dog's leash, he moved up to the ticket window.

"Gimme two round trips," he said to the girl inside and placed a bill on the counter. A large bill, because she picked it up and studied it.

I hoped it was counterfeit. I hoped she'd call the

5

police, and they'd lock up Carl Hayes for the rest of the summer. How could the Ballous have rented their house to a man like that?

The girl in the booth counted out his change and handed him the tickets.

The child in the stroller began to whimper.

Both parents glanced at her, and then Dorothy Hayes stared at me again.

"Say, maybe you know some kid who can baby-sit for us tonight. We need to get out."

"Ask Scotty," I said. "Scotty Banks. The young man who gives the kids swimming lessons. Scotty lines up sitters for everybody."

I picked up my bundles, walked to the ticket window, and asked for the summer ferry schedules for Sharon's Landing and Fair Harbor and the schedule for the lateral ferry. Dorothy and Carl Hayes disappeared inside the waiting area bordering the ferry docks, and I forgot about them. I had other things on my mind.

Though the ferries weren't due to leave for half an hour, the waiting area was full of people. Most of them, it seemed, came in pairs—just to remind me that Henry was dead, that I was going to Fire Island without him, going out for the first time since he died, last August, when he skidded into a stalled trailer-truck on the thruway driving home from Albany in the middle of the night in the middle of a thunderstorm. I wallowed in self-pity for almost three minutes, asking myself, as I did at least ten times a day, why he was driving so fast in all that rain. Why couldn't he have stopped at the restaurant at the Suffern turnoff and had a cup of coffee and waited for the heavy rain to let up? Then I squeezed into an empty space on one of the molded benches by the water, settling the dog on my lap and the lobsters and groceries between my feet.

Ignoring the couple on my right (his jean-encased leg

pressed against hers), I looked into the canal at the comforting shapes of the six ferries—six old friends. The *Captain Patterson*, a large white wedding cake of a boat—its top deck enclosed with a metal grillwork that sparkled in the sunlight—carried the crowds back and forth to Ocean Beach. The *Traveler* or the *Fire Island Miss* would take us to Sharon's Landing by way of Kismet, or Dunewood, or both—unless they gave us one of the small boats all to ourselves (the *Firefly*, the *Fire Islander*, and the *Isle of Fire* were waiting now). In high season, the boats served as lateral ferries as well, connecting the string of western communities with Ocean Beach and traveling all the way east to Cherry Grove on weekend nights. All six boats were empty now, deserted by their crews, bobbing lightly alongside their docks.

Barely noticing the couple on my left (shoulder-to-shoulder over the *New York Review of Books*), I glanced back through the wide entryway by the ticket window to the front of the terminal. A man, a woman, and two teenage girls were unloading their Volvo, piling suitcases and canvas totes on the walk by the curb. When they finished, the woman drove across the asphalt square and parked in the lot behind the freight house, while the man and girls carried their things to a bench inside the waiting area. They'd carry them onto the ferry in a little while and then off again, at their dock on Fire Island, and then load them on a red children's wagon and pull them all the way to their house. These rituals give most of us pleasure—in spite of the work they put us to—for we count it among our blessings that Fire Island has no streets for cars to run on, only walkways for wagons and bicycles and barefoot pedestrians.

A black mini-bus, one of the direct-service jitneys from Manhattan, pulled in where the Volvo had been and discharged its passengers: three men in city suits and ties; a woman with a small baby; and a couple, about my age. I looked away quickly and focused on a small boy, inside the waiting area, making his way in my general direction. He was about the size of Woody, my own eleven-year-old, though thinner and frailer, with dark copper hair. I didn't know him, and he glanced at me without recognition, but his pensive face brightened when he saw Mops on my lap. He hurried over and put out his hand, inviting the dog to lick it. Mops obliged, thumping his tail on the top of my thigh.

The boy raised his head. "Where's Woody? Didn't he come with you?"

"Woody's at tennis camp. For three weeks." I smiled at him, hoping he'd smile back. He didn't. "Say," I said, pretending to study him, "don't you have a house in Sharon's Landing?"

He nodded, still solemn.

"A two-story house?"

He nodded again, his sad brown eyes beginning to shine.

"And a lot of fishing poles and a cook who makes the best brownies in the world?" I snapped my fingers. "I've got it! You're Jimmy Milgrim!"

He smiled with pleasure, revealing an arsenal of braces. Each tooth wore its own corrective hardware; wires stretched across uppers and lowers, and there were hooks all over the place for a night brace and rubber bands.

I put out my hand. "I'm glad to meet you, Jimmy." We shook on it. "Where's your family?" Ten months ago, the Milgrims had bought the house right behind mine. I'd never seen them, but Jimmy and Woody had met when Woody and my two daughters came out to Fire Island together last Labor Day weekend to close the house for the season.

"Are your mother and father here?" I asked.

Jimmy's smile faded. "He's my stepfather." He spit

out the word. "He's not coming to Sharon's Landing until tomorrow night. He just rode out with us to the ferry. Him and my mother are over there."

"He," I corrected automatically.

Jimmy motioned through the entryway to a white Mercedes backed up to the curb. A slight man in blue-tinted sunglasses, with thin gray hair, was helping his chauffeur unload. This was Leo Milgrim—a trial lawyer, and a distinguished one, according to my brother, George, an assistant district attorney in Manhattan. The woman who leaned against a post watching the two men was, I assumed, June Milgrim. Only her husband and son knew for sure. She hid her body inside a baggy sweat-shirt and shapeless slacks, covered her hair with a ban-dana, and masked her face with a large beach hat and a huge pair of sunglasses.

"Mrs. Lambert," Jimmy said anxiously, "when you write to Woody, will you tell him something?"

I nodded.

"Tell him that Scotty Banks lives at my Fire Island house!" He straightened his shoulders and took a deep breath. "My mother's paying him to stay with us and take me swimming and sailing and stuff in his spare time!" Jimmy nodded toward the Mercedes. "*He* didn't like the idea, and they had a big fight about it, but my mother won!" He grinned triumphantly, flashing his hardware. "Scotty and I go swimming in the ocean, and he hits tennis balls with me, and he's even going to teach me how to play chess! Now you tell Woody!"

I promised I would.

A deckhand unlatched the wooden gate to the dock at the far end of the bulkhead. "Ocean Beach! Ocean Beach!" he called. "Have your tickets ready!"

A second deckhand jumped to the dock off the top deck of the *Fire Island Miss*. "Fair Harbor! Fair Harbor only!" he called, opening the gate.

People around me stood up and collected their belongings and their children and their dogs.

I needed company rather badly now. Attaching the dog's leash, I strolled over to the crowd by the third gate and looked for someone I knew among the eighty or ninety passengers waiting to board the *Traveler*. A lot of people from our commune of pleasure manage to make the early boat on Friday afternoon. But I didn't see a single familiar face—especially not Will Mortimer's. An orthopedic surgeon, Will almost always closed up shop at one. He was an old friend; I had counted on riding with him out to Sharon's Landing. Or with Paula Wohlens, one of my tennis cronies. Paula was an economist who started each weekend on Friday, because the mayor or somebody in Washington always seemed to need her on Sunday afternoon.

So I got in line alone and waited for the gate to open. The couple next to me wore identical backpacks; he whispered something in her ear. With a sigh, I put down my packages and picked up the dog, who was whining again.

"Kismet and Sharon's Landing! This way!" A deckhand opened the gate.

I stooped for my tote and the lobsters, and I was reaching for the shopping bag when the Hayes's German shepherd lunged from behind and knocked it over. A box of blueberries broke open at my feet. A bunch of broccoli and a dozen pumpernickel rolls skidded out on the dock.

"Stupid dog!" Carl Hayes reined in the slack leash, jerked savagely at the dog's collar, and walked by me, avoiding a smashed tomato, but stepping (deliberately, I thought) on the watercress.

I didn't say a word or try to stop him. I'm not a foolhardy woman. I put my lobsters and the dog on a bench by the gate and salvaged a second tomato, a jar of homemade mayonnaise, and a slice of country pâté, wrapped in aluminum foil. Out on the dock ten feet away, I saw Will Mortimer collecting pumpernickel rolls and dropping them in his doctor's bag. He rescued the broccoli and wove back through the crowd—a tall, lanky, loose-limbed man with light brown hair just beginning to turn gray (though he was fifty-two or fifty-three) and skin tanned almost the same color. He wore a blue nylon windbreaker the color of his eyes, a pair of faded jeans, and ancient sneakers without socks.

He stuffed the broccoli into my tote and opened his bag. "Some of your rolls fell in the water. But I rescued eight of them," he drawled, his Arkansas country-boy accent blurred but not abandoned after twenty-five years in the East. "They're only a little dirty." He picked out a roll and wiped it on his jeans. "Go ahead and serve them to company. I won't tell." He grinned. "Lily!" His grin widened. "How are you?"

Before I could answer, he bent down, eight inches worth, and kissed me on my cheek. My left cheek. He meant it to be an affectionate greeting from one friend to another. But it didn't work out that way. I couldn't believe how good it made me feel. I thought he ought to kiss me on the right cheek, just to balance things out. I wondered how it would feel if he kissed me on the mouth and on the side of my neck, just above the collarbone.

"It's good to have you back," he said warmly and patted my shoulder.

He picked up my bag of lobsters, handed me the dog, and took my arm. I floated beside him out onto the dock.

The breeze blowing in from the bay cooled me off in a hurry—even before Will said, "There's Caroline," and nodded toward his honey-haired wife, who was stepping on board the ferry.

The *Traveler* was a large ferry with tan molded benches, wide aisles, and dozens of shiny red life jackets decorating the overhead.

"Come sit with us," Will invited.

I swallowed and forced myself to say "No, thanks. I need some sun. I'm going topside."

But I had to pass his wife, who'd commandeered half a tan bench between the stairways that led to the upper deck. And I couldn't go by without stopping to say hello and kiss the cheek she offered and ask, "How was your winter?"

This was not a request for information, but a ritual greeting, exchanged by Fire Islanders who hadn't seen each other since they closed their houses after Labor Day. Anyone else who'd had a bad winter would have replied, "I've seen better," or maybe "I'm surviving," and save the details for a private moment.

But not Caroline Mortimer. "Terrible!" she groaned. "I can't tell you how terrible!" She rolled her large lavender eyes up to the overhead.

I'd had a pretty rotten winter myself, but I asked, "What happened, Caroline?"

"Didn't anyone tell you about Millie?"

I shook my head.

"Millie walked out on us," she drawled dramatically. "Last fall. Right before she was supposed to start college. We haven't seen her since!"

"But why—"

"Scotty Banks, that's why." Her voice was harsh and bitter. "He dropped her cold. That bastard treated my daughter like she was dirt!"

A woman with curly salt-and-pepper hair called, "Caroline," from the far aisle. She wore a black tank top and a black gauze skirt with a string of fringe on the hem that skimmed the top of her rubber thongs. Her toenails were painted green.

"Don't forget tomorrow. Can you leave at seven-thirty?" she asked.

Caroline rose and went over to talk to her. Which left me with Will again.

"I'm sorry about Millie," I said stiffly.

"It's not as bad as Caroline makes it sound." He shook his head and added, "Not quite as bad, anyway. We've heard from her. She's okay, we think. But she won't come home." Then he studied my face as if he were trying to read my thoughts.

"See you later," I said hastily and escaped up the stairs to a bench behind the pilot's house on the top deck.

Now I pride myself on being a rational woman—clear-eyed, judicious—except, of course, when my feelings get in the way. I frowned and shifted around the dog on my lap and faced the problem: the fact is, I'm lonesome. Especially in the morning when I still grind twice as many coffee beans as I can use. Especially at night. Lonesome enough to lose my head, act like a lost puppy, and wag my tail at an old friend—an old married friend like Will Mortimer.

The engines throbbed below, drowning out for a moment the clatter of my conscience. Deckhands scurried to untie the ropes. As the ferry backed away from the dock and moved slowly through the widening canal, I promised myself (and Caroline, in absentia) that Will Mortimer would never, ever warm my cockles! Then the captain turned the engines on full, and the boat leaped forward into Great South Bay.

It was a perfect beauty of a day—cool, dry, salt-scented. A crisp north breeze cleared the sky of clouds and sent the waves skittering ahead of the ferry. Markers, bell-buoys, and flat-bottomed clam boats at anchor rocked and swayed in the choppy water, and a pair of Sunfish dipped their sails almost horizontal. To the east, a large charter filled with fishermen pitched in the wake of a cabin cruiser. And to the south, half an hour's ride from the mainland, Fire Island floated on the edge of the horizon. A long, thin, fragile sand bar dotted with summer houses, it shimmered like a satin ribbon in the sunlight.

Twenty minutes out, we skirted the largest of the Bay Islands and a dozen fishing charters at anchor in the waters between Kismet and the old lighthouse. The captain slowed his engines and maneuvered through the channel to the Kismet dock. Most of the passengers disembarked, emptying the upper deck, revealing the travelers bound for Sharon's Landing: two couples I didn't know and John Wohlens, four rows back, his cold pipe in his mouth (smoking wasn't permitted on the ferries), attempting to read the *Wall Street Journal*. He had opened the paper to its midsection, and it was fluttering in the wind like a huge butterfly.

Our ferry moved away from the dock and headed east.

I stood up and collected my creatures. As I made my way to the middle aisle, John rose to greet me—a tall man, taller than Will, in his early forties, with thick, shiny dark hair rumpled by the wind and a long, elegant, upper-class English face. If John had been an actor, instead of an obscure political science professor at an obscure community college in New Jersey, he could have auditioned for all the Rex Harrison parts.

"Welcome back, Lily." He stuffed the newspaper into his briefcase, tucked his pipe into the pocket of his brown tweed jacket, and leaned down to kiss me.

I felt his lips brush my cheek. Nothing happened. No palpitations; not even a pleasant glow. I was a different woman this time. But then John was a different man— colorless as a quahog clam in spite of his glossy looks, and dull, without a trace of humor, even when he talked politics. He almost never smiled, but he was smiling now, his long, aristocratic face beaming.

He straightened up and took his pipe out of his pocket.

It's rumored in Sharon's Landing that he sleeps with it.
"Long time no see. How are you feeling?"

"Fine," I said brightly. "Just fine. Where's Paula?"

"At the beach already. He placed his pipe back in his
mouth and held it there lightly, with his fingertips. "She
flew in this morning. Have you seen her lately?"

"Not for a couple of months."

"I think she's worn out. She needs a lot of fresh air
and tennis." He sounded almsot parental in his concern
for her. Usually it was the other way around. Paula
always fussed over John as if he were a child.

"Oh, Lily, I bought a new racquet." He took it off the
seat and removed its cover. "What do you think of it?"
He handed it to me.

It was a top-of-the-line Prince, big and light, and it felt
wonderful in my hand. "Wow," I breathed.

"It was expensive, I admit." He took it back from me,
zipped it in its cover again, and put it under his arm.
"But I needed a new racquet. And I'm playing in a
tournament next week." He shrugged. "We only live
once, don't we?"

He picked up his briefcase and a small cardboard
pastry box tied with string and marked William Greenberg, Jr. Desserts," took my arm the way Will had (are
most widows halt and blind, I wondered?), and led me
down the aisle. At the head of the stairs, I retrieved my
arm and urged him to go below without me. I decided to
stay on the open deck a few more minutes. "Until I can
see my house," I explained.

The ferry ran parallel to the Fire Island bayfront until
it was directly opposite Sharon's Landing. As it turned
south, a seaplane, settling on the bay to the east,
skimmed toward the dock, riding on its pontoons like a
water skier. The boat slowed almost to a halt, waiting for
the plane to tie up at the dock and let off its passengers. I
could guess who they were: Brian and Jo-Ellen Mac-

Kay's Wall Street law firm was a ten-minute taxi ride from the seaplane terminal in the East River. The Mac-Kays flew out whenever they could; it was an extravagance, but the trip, dock to dock, took them about twenty minutes.

We were still too far away to see the people at the bayfront waiting for our arrival. But I could make out a patch of light green—the three tennis courts—over the tops of the dark green pine trees planted as windbreaks. I could find fragments of the three crosswalks and the three bay-to-ocean walkways. And I could count off all twenty houses (though some showed only a corner or a bit of roof). They started out fifteen years ago as tract houses raised above the bare sand on skinny locust posts—each with the same three-bedroom, open-kitchen plan, with sliding-glass doors out to a cedar deck and a cedar ramp leading down to one of the walkways. Then only the color of each—blue, yellow, white, green or pink—set it apart from its neighbors. But over the years they'd been altered and added to, landscaped with pine trees, Russian olive, beach plum, and bright beds of flowers, outfitted with bicycle racks and storage sheds, extended with bedrooms and extra decks. The former owners of the Milgrim house even built on a second story.

Six houses clustered behind the sliver of sand on our bay beach; ten more climbed the gently sloping land on the other side of Center Walk, and four others—silhouetted now against the sky—sat on the crest of dune overlooking the ocean.

The seaplane left the dock and taxied east. The ferry began to move—slowly, inching cautiously between the markers in the shallow channel. I watched our approach a minute longer and then descended the stairs, joining John Wohlens, who was standing with the Mortimers behind the crowd at the exit door.

16

We were close enough now to see a pair of young boys fishing off the end of the dock—the d'Angelo twins, buddies of my eleven-year-old son. Just behind the twins, Paula Wohlens, a small, chestnut-haired woman in sneakers and a rumpled tennis dress, searched for John among the faces on the ferry. Two tall, thin, bikini-clad women waved at the two couples on the upper deck. Both women pulled empty red children's wagons for their visitors' luggage.

To the right of the dock, a mother's helper watched her charge playing on the tiny beach, in front of the roped-off area of the bay where Scotty Banks was teaching a swimming class. Behind Scotty, twenty feet out from the diving raft, half a dozen people stood hip-deep on the flats, bent over slightly, clamming with their toes.

I felt like hugging them all. God's in his heaven, I thought. At least this little corner of it.

Scotty Banks, shepherding his class to shore, loped across the sand and leaped up onto the dock. Rubbing the palms of his hands over his wet auburn hair, he smiled, it seemed to me, at everything around him—at the arrival of the ferry, the familiar faces on board, the magnificent weather, the great good luck of being a healthy, uncommonly handsome young man of twenty-one and having the great good fortune to be spending the summer on Fire Island.

A deckhand unlatched the exit door. Jimmy Milgrim, pushing his way between the grown-ups, flew out of the ferry and threw his arms around Scotty's wet waist.

"Hey there, Jimmy!" The young man hugged the boy around the shoulders. "How was the city? Did the dentist treat you right?"

"Oh, Scotty!" the boy said fiercely. "I missed you so all week!"

"Hi, Scotty!" June Milgrim smiled at the young man, as happy to see him as her son was. Happier, maybe.

She'd come out of hiding. Hatless, scarfless, the baggy sweatshirt discarded and the sunglasses pushed up through her gleaming copper hair, she was a beautiful woman.

We stopped moving. A nervous young couple, coping with a huge English baby carriage, blocked the exit. Out on the dock, June and Scotty shook hands a long time, beaming at each other as if they hadn't met for a year.

Caroline Mortimer, standing next to me, muttered, "Look at him with that woman. Look at him!" Her voice rose. "He'd better watch out," she drawled, reckless, not caring who heard her. "One of these days I'm going to kill that—"

"Shut up!" Will hissed, angrier than I'd ever seen him. "Mind your own business!"

"Since when isn't it my business?" she retorted. "Or yours?"

The baby carriage landed safely, and we moved forward.

"Careful, now." John Wohlens helped me down the six-inch step to the dock before walking over to join his wife.

Paula Wohlens pushed her shabby chestnut bangs off her forehead, reached up, and put her arms around her husband's neck.

John took his pipe out of his mouth, leaned down, and kissed her. Then he replaced his pipe and reached in his pocket for his lighter. "Did you bring the wagon?" I heard him ask.

I attached the dog's leash, pulled off my sneakers and socks, and strolled out to the end of the dock to visit with the d'Angelo twins. I admired the weakfish in their pail. "How was your winter?" I asked.

I should have enjoyed myself then. I should have curled my toes on the cool wood slats of the dock and watched the waves lap at the bulkhead and rock the speedboats in the slips. I should have listened for the boom of the ocean hidden behind the dunes a hundred yards to the south. And then I should have started for home, up Blueberry, where the pine trees had grown a foot since last July and the flower beds were bright with yellow pansies. But I stood there, unable to move, weeping over Henry and feeling utterly abandoned without him.

Mops tugged at the leash, and I turned and watched the last few people leave the dock. June Milgrim and Jimmy strolled off with Scotty Banks, who pulled a wagon filled with grocery bags and a Gucci tote. John and Paula Wohlens walked in silence—John smoking his pipe. Will and Caroline Mortimer, still bristling at each other, maneuvered their wagon onto Blueberry.

Dorothy and Carl Hayes were the last to leave. He held the German shepherd by its collar. The dog bared its teeth and growled at a seagull on the bulkhead.

"Shut up," Carl muttered.

That was the beginning.

II
Saturday, July 2

2

MOPS RAISED HIS head off the pillow of my sneakers and growled at the voices on the beach stairs.

Surfcasters, I guessed. Or early morning joggers, going home, for it was six-thirty already. I had overslept. Too bad. I felt as logy as a waterlogged rope. Dragging myself out of bed, I padded into the kitchen to plug in the coffee pot and padded back to the bedroom to pull on a pair of shorts and a tennis shirt. If I hadn't taken a sleeping pill, I would have been up at sunrise—in plenty of time to be sitting out on my deck with a book when Will Mortimer climbed the beach stairs after he finished jogging. Too bad. He would have invited himself up for a cup of coffee—the way he used to do, every weekend morning last summer, whenever he saw us sitting outside—Henry and me.

I sighed and smeared my face with sunblock and stepped out on the deck to look at the morning. It was glorious—cool and dry, with a light, fresh breeze off the water. The grass-covered dune beyond the deck railing sloped gently to the white beach thirty feet below. The beach was abandoned, now, except for a woman and a child strolling on the hard sand by the shoreline. Beyond them, the vast, empty Atlantic, ruffled by the breeze, shimmered in the slanting sunlight. It was low tide. A lazy surf swelled and retreated, muttering softly. Just right for swimming, even for a coward like me. I'll go down to the beach this afternoon, I promised myself—

and so will everyone else, I thought, even devoted tennis players like Taki Andreapolis and Will Mortimer.

Suddenly I felt a lot better.

Mops whined and scratched at the door. I fastened his leash and led him down the ramp and across Ocean Walk to one of the brand new Japanese pine trees in the Milgrims' front yard. It was at least six feet tall, and there were half a dozen others, providing instant privacy for the first floor. Privacy, I noticed, wasn't quite such a concern for the second-story bedroom. Maybe June Milgrim thought nobody looked up, for she hadn't bothered to draw the curtains across the floor-to-ceiling windows.

I led the dog east to Beach Plum Walk. We turned the corner, and I stopped to admire Elmo Kesselbaum's new back deck, twice as large as the old one, with built-in flower boxes spilling white petunias over the railing. Elmo's house fit snugly on top of a secondary dune, except for the new deck, which hung out in the air, perched on a dozen spindly locust posts rising out of the sand and the patches of poison ivy in the yard below. I moved a few steps down Beach Plum and peered at the mess underneath the deck—broken boards from the old deck, saved for firewood and stacked untidily behind the first row of locust posts; a cracked toilet; and an old red wagon, overturned, lying on its back in the poison ivy like a dead animal, its rusty wheels held stiffly in the air. Elmo had planted a hedge of junipers to screen the area from the walk and from the Ballous' side deck next door. But they were too small and too skimpy to do the job. He could afford to add some pine trees, I thought, and glanced across the junipers to Blueberry and the side of the Milgrim house, where Al Fry was stalking a bird.

Al is a painter. In a self-portrait that hangs in his Fire Island house, he sketched himself with absolute accuracy as a bunch of circles—rotund body, moon-shaped

24

face, round eyes framed by the circular metal frames of his glasses. Al and his wife Cissy, who are old friends of mine from the city, had eaten lobster at my house the night before. This morning, Al was peering through his binoculars at a bird in one of the Milgrims' pine trees. The bird flew away, and I would have called out a greeting, if I hadn't been afraid of waking up a couple of households. And if Al hadn't turned suddenly and trained his binoculars on June Milgrim's second-floor bedroom.

"What's he doing?" I muttered, like a fool. But Al Fry simply couldn't be an ordinary Peeping Tom. He painted the female figure, unclothed, from live models. Why should he stalk, on the sly, what he stared at legitimately, hour after hour, all week long in his studio?

I couldn't think of any answer that was good for Cissy.

Al lowered his binoculars carefully, with both hands, as if they contained some fragile, precious vision, and walked down Blueberry toward the bay.

"Come on, Mops!" I tugged roughly on the leash. He whimpered in surprise and let me lead him down Beach Plum.

Scotty Banks had just unlocked the gate to the tennis courts. I was going to catch up with him and visit a little. But I stopped in front of the Ballous' house across from the courts because Katie Huff came out the front door. Katie is ten years old and no early riser; at 6:45 in the morning, she should have been home in her bed in the green house on Holly Walk.

She was crying.

Scotty, still holding his ball cage and racquets, came over to the foot of the Ballous' ramp. "What's the matter, Katie? What are you doing here?"

"I just finished baby-sitting, that's what!" she sobbed. "I had to sit all night! They said they'd come home early from Ocean Beach, but they didn't come home until just now." She sniffed and wiped her nose on the sleeve of her sweatshirt. "Mrs. Hayes went right into the bedroom and fell asleep with all her clothes on. And Mr. Hayes told me to come back later for my money because all he had was a fifty-dollar bill!"

"Won't your mother be worried?" I asked.

"It's Grandma. Mom's in Italy. Grandma said she was going to wait up until I came home but she probably fell asleep on the couch."

The door to the blue house opened. Mops growled and then hid behind my legs as the German shepherd trotted down the ramp, crossed the walk, and urinated against the new bicycle rack in front of the Mortimers' pink house.

Carl Hayes stood in the doorway, bleary-eyed, shirtless, his fat white belly rolling over the top of his jeans. He held out a bill to Katie. "Here you are, kid. Twenty bucks," he said loudly, looking at us. "My wife says give you twenty bucks."

"Take it, Katie," Scotty said, "and run on home."

She sniffed and put the bill in the pocket of her jeans and hurried down the ramp and around the corner.

"Mr. Hayes," Scotty said sternly, "your wife told me you'd be home early, or I never would have asked Katie to sit for you. She's only ten years old. You have no right to keep a child that age up all night."

"Who says so?" Carl sneered.

"Come on, Scotty." I put my hand on his arm. I saw Taki Andreapolis turn the corner by Elmo Kesselbaum's house. "Let's go to the courts. Taki's coming."

Scotty shook off my hand. "*I* say so, Mr. Hayes."

"Want to make something of it, Pretty Boy?" Carl hitched up his jeans and started down the ramp.

His face flushed with anger, Scotty set his racquets and ball cage in the middle of the walk and strode over to meet Carl.

"Stop it!" I said sharply. "Taki's here."

As Scotty glanced up Beach Plum, so did Carl, who stopped moving. He had second thoughts about fighting Scotty with Taki looking over his shoulder—and I didn't blame him a bit. Taki Andreapolis wouldn't raise his hand to squash a mosquito, but Carl didn't know that—and Taki does look dangerous. Though only my height—five-six—he's heavily muscled, with the large chest and strong arms of a wrestler. A throwback, I like to think, to some Olympian ancestor.

Carl snapped his fingers for the dog, who trotted up the ramp and into the house. His owner followed, slamming the door behind him.

I began to breathe again.

"Next time I see that son-of-a-bitch, I'll . . ."

"You won't do anything," I said sharply. "He's twice your size and a hundred times meaner. Why, he could kill you."

Taki caught up with us. "You're early," he said to Scotty. "My watch says ten of."

He was carrying two classic wood racquets and wearing classic tennis whites. His pristine shirt—unadorned by even a small navy Polo player over the heart—set off his dark, sculpted features and black curly hair. "Hi, Lily." He nodded mechanically, not really seeing me, since I didn't figure in his tennis plans this morning. Taki is a child psychiatrist, a fact that usually slips my mind because on weekends he lives and breathes only tennis. (Last spring, when he snapped his Achilles tendon and couldn't play for a month, he took up fishing with the same single-minded fervor.)

He switched his racquets to the other shoulder. "Let's start the lesson now, Scotty, and I'll pay you for extra time."

I watched them cross Center Walk and open the gate to the courts. Then I went home to breakfast.

27

An hour later, I rode down to the courts on my bike for my eight-o'clock game.

Inside, on the singles court, Scotty was playing a set with Taki. I watched him pass the older man on his backhand, grin triumphantly, and trot back to the baseline loose and easy. From now on, I thought, with his swimming classes at the bay and his tennis clinics at the courts, he'll be too busy to get into trouble with Carl Hayes.

I walked over to the bench by the first doubles court, where Paula Wohlens was sitting, reading a book, and Cissy Fry was standing, studying the schedule of court assignments tacked up on the fence. From the back, in her skivvy top and the accordion-pleated tennis skirt that rippled over her small, tight rump, Cissy looked like a dancer ready to go on the stage in a tennis costume. Like a young dancer, I marveled, with a twenty-two-inch waist and a pair of legs as sleek and graceful as they were fifteen years ago, when she was forty. When she gave up dancing and took up tennis.

"Good morning, Lily." Cissy's accent was pure Milwaukee. She sat down on the bench, crossed her long, lovely legs, and yawned. "Sorry," she said, a tired smile on her plain, middle-aged face, "but Al woke me at six to pack a lunch for him. I know that's not early for you, but I read half the night! He's out in his boat. For the whole day." She yawned again. "He's after migratory birds."

The kind that roost in second-floor bedrooms, I thought, and wondered whether Cissy suspected anything. She seemed kind of testy and strained.

"Here comes the lady in white." Cissy nodded toward the gate. "In full regalia."

Sharon Jessup's milky skin burned and blistered even in the shade at Fire Island. She protected herself by never going swimming (no real hardship; Sharon didn't know how) and by staying in the house unless she was completely covered. She dressed for tennis in loose white slacks, long-sleeved turtleneck shirt, tennis hat, sunglasses, and thick waterproof opaque makeup on top of the layer of sun-block that covered her face and neck and the backs of her hands.

Sharon ambled over to the bench, sipping coffee from a big Snoopy mug. She watched the two men for a minute and then placed her mug under the bench and opened a new can of heavy-duty balls. "Let's go," she said.

We four are strong, skillful players, and though we're evenly matched, each of us has a specialty. Who's best at what isn't hard to guess, if you know us. Sharon covers the court fast as lightning, slacks flapping, platinum-blonde ponytail bouncing on the back of her turtleneck. She worked up her speed, she claims, running after three small children at home. Paula Wohlens has the best ground strokes. She practiced them and perfected them almost as carefully as she prepared her doctoral thesis and her proposals to the mayor for fiscal reform. Our most cerebral player, she anticipates and plans her shots with uncanny speed. Cissy Fry, with the strong, supple back of an ex-dancer, has the most effective serve—bullet hard, deadly accurate—and an overhead slam that destroys us. I'm a terror at net—at interfering with the plans of my opponents, intercepting their wickedest shots, saving the game for the good guys.

Cissy and I won the first set from the two younger women and would have won the second, if I hadn't lost my concentration.

When it was all over and we came off the court, I collapsed on the bench.

"You blew it." Cissy wiped her face and her short gray hair with one of the blue-rimmed towels she always brings.

"Sorry." I sighed. "All of a sudden, I forgot how to play the game."

Sharon studied the sign-up sheet. "We'll give you another chance this afternoon. What's better for you— three o'clock or four?"

"Four is better. It's going to be *hot* today."

They all nodded, and Sharon wrote in our names. Then she lifted the Saturday sign-up sheet and looked at Sunday. "How's eight o'clock for tomorrow?"

Paula shook her head. "I won't be here. We're going back to the city tonight, on the eight-twenty-five ferry. John has to catch the first train to Philadelphia Sunday morning. Imagine!"

"I'll put down Edna for our fourth." Sharon wrote in the names and then bent down for her coffee mug. "Somebody call her?" Cissy nodded. "I have to get home in a hurry. It's the dog; he's running a fever again." She frowned, cracking her makeup. "If my kids were sick as often as he is, I'd go crazy."

"Coming, Lily?" Paula asked.

"As soon as I can stand up again." I fanned myself with my tennis hat. "I took a sleeping pill last night, and it knocked me out. I don't really take them anymore, but it was two in the morning, and I'd been tossing and turning for a couple of hours, and I'd brought along the bottle of Halcion just in case. So I popped one. I wish I hadn't. You know," I added, "I haven't played tennis for ten months! Not since Henry died," I said, almost choking on the words.

Paula leaned her racquet against the fence and sat down next to me.

"Still seeing the shrink?" she asked.

"For a little while longer," I admitted. "I still have a few things to work out." Just a few, I told myself: insomnia, depression, fear of heights, fear of dying.

"Seven. Eight." Cissy was doing pliés behind the bench. "Good Lord, Paula, when are you going to get rid of that tennis dress? It's ready for the rag pile."

"When I have time," she said patiently. "I planned to buy two or three tennis dresses this spring, only—"

"Only you were too busy," Cissy said. "Eleven. Twelve. And you need a haircut, too."

"I know." Paula pushed back her bangs again. "I really haven't had a minute to spare. I had to be in Washington and Albany twice as often as last year—and I've been driving out to Pennsylvania to spend the weekend with John whenever the mayor doesn't need me; it's a long drive—four and a half hours each way."

"What's John doing in Pennsylvania?" I asked.

"I didn't say a word!" Cissy centered her body, pulled in her stomach, and descended slowly. "I promised you I wouldn't tell her!"

"Tell me what?"

Paula's eyes, limpid and glowing, prepared me for good news about John. About a job change, of course, since he changed every couple of years. This time, though, he must have moved up in the academic world, instead of down or sideways.

"John has a new job. At Lynfield College in Pennsylvania—about two hours west of Philadelphia. And it's not a teaching job. They've made him acting president!"

"Oh, Paula!" I put my arms around her and hugged her tight. "When did it happen?"

"Six weeks ago." She looked as pleased and happy as I'd ever seen her. "It's just a tiny college, of course; most people never heard of it. But it's John's alma mater, and they love him. He's one of their few graduates with a genuine doctorate, and he's been a trustee forever. He's only acting president, now, but that's supposed to change to the real thing some time in the fall."

"I can just picture him as a college president," I said. He really did look the part. Maybe, I thought, John's finally found his niche.

"Twenty-five pliés," Cissy said. "That's enough for

now." She came around and joined us on the bench. She'd do twenty-five more by evening, plus an hour of ballet warmups, stretches, and special exercises. If she was ever asked to fill in at the New York City Ballet, she'd be ready.

Four men were still playing on Court Two. Will Mortimer was one. Will, usually a solid, steady player, was sending all his backhand shots into the net.

"Your old friend Will isn't playing too well," Cissy murmured. "Or didn't you notice, Lily?"

I grabbed her towel and tossed it to her. "Let's get out of here."

3

"WHAT DO YOU say, Lily?" Bo Jessup, the founding father of Sharon's Landing, folded his freckled arms across his freckled chest and beamed at me like the host at a very good party. "How do you like that ocean?" he marveled, boasting a little, as if he'd ordered it.

A band of warm, green water from the Gulf Stream invaded our coast at noontime, turning our portion of the chilly blue Atlantic into a Caribbean sea. It had never happened before—and everyone came down to the beach to marvel at it. So many people were swimming or floating on the gentle swells or visiting with each other waist-deep in the clear, tepid, tropical water, that the lifeguard climbed down from his stand and stood watch right at the shoreline.

"Quite a crowd, isn't it?" Bo Jessup surveyed the swimmers proudly. He had, in a sense, brought them there. He had built all the houses in Sharon's Landing, laid out the walks, constructed the tennis courts, and even named the place—sentimentalist that he was, and is—after his wife. The irony of naming a Fire Island community after a woman who couldn't swim, or get a suntan, or ride a bike, occurs to me periodically.

I waded into the ocean and paddled around. I admitted to myself that I was looking for Will. I had given up and was heading back to the beach when I finally saw him, knee-high in the water near the shore, waiting for me to catch up with him.

"Careful there," he warned. A large jellyfish pulsed

between us, tentacles streaming behind it like a woman's hair. We watched it pass.

Will moved closer. "Where were you this morning? I expected to be invited up for a cup of coffee when I finished jogging."

"I overslept. But I won't oversleep tomorrow," I said eagerly. Too eagerly. "I hate to miss the best part of the day," I added quickly, avoiding his eyes.

"The sunrise was a beauty. I hope it's as nice tomorrow." He spoke lightly, one old friend to another. Then we both looked out into the deep water, where his wife, Caroline, was swimming back and forth parallel to the shoreline, swimming laps in a phantom pool.

Bo Jessup, wading through the whisper of a surf, clapped a freckled hand on Will's shoulder. "I been looking for you, Will. I want to ask you something." He cleared his throat. "Lily, it's kind of private, if you don't mind."

I went for another swim, hoping, when I returned, that Bo had moved on. But he was still talking to Will. I decided to leave the beach. It was time to change for my four o'clock tennis game.

Caroline Mortimer called out "Lily! I need to talk to you!" and ran to catch up with me, her honey-colored hair streaming behind her. She was a Brunhild of a woman—tall, fair, regal, dramatically beautiful, even in her damp, blue-denim work shirt buttoned wrong over a black tank suit; even though she was a little too thick around the waist this summer, and a lot too tense.

"I have the most marvelous thing to tell you!" She tapped me on the shoulder as if she were awarding me a prize. "Five of us started a women's group out here. You know. For consciousness-raising. We've met every Saturday night since the first of June, and I can't tell you how it's helped me. Before then, I was absolutely climbing the wall about my daughter. And my father." She put her hand on the railing of the beach stairs, rolled her eyes up to the sky, and announced, "My father died two months ago."

"Oh, Caroline, I'm so sorry."

Her face brightened; she looked almost happy as we climbed the beach stairs.

"Anyway, the good news is, we want you to join our group."

"No, thank you." I shook my head. "I just can't do it." I really couldn't. Talking with my analyst was hard enough.

"Of course you can!" She gave me her velvety smile and blinked long, mascara-darkened lashes over her large lavender eyes (once upon a time, I imagined, that smile and those blinks enslaved half the male population of Fayetteville, Arkansas).

"Why don't you ask Paula?"

"We already did—though it wasn't my idea. Paula refused us, I'm glad to say. For a smart woman, she's awfully dumb. All I ever hear from her is how John's going to do this or John's going to do that."

"What about Sharon?"

"Not on your life," Caroline said coldly. "She has too many problems; we'd never have time for anyone else. We want you, Lily. We're thinking of your welfare. You need to talk out your feelings about Henry's death and about other men."

"No!" I looked away and swallowed and said, "I just can't, Caroline."

"Well, think about it. We'll talk again," she added brusquely and dismissed me with a regal wave.

I showered quickly, pulled on a tennis shirt and shorts, and took the dog out for a walk. Just as I was passing the beach stairs, Will Mortimer climbed the last two steps, carrying a towel and a book and his straw beach mat rolled up and tucked under his arm.

"Lily!" His face lit up. "I'm dying for a cup of coffee. How about making me one after you walk the dog?"

"I can't, Will. There isn't time. I'm playing tennis at four."

"Oh, well." He grinned. "I'm supposed to go clamming, anyway. After I drop this stuff at the house." He switched the beach mat to his other arm and strolled beside me, down Blueberry. "Caroline needs two dozen for her women's group tonight. I suppose I ought to get started."

But he didn't. Instead of turning east at Center to go to his house, he crossed the walk with me and stopped when I stopped to let the dog sniff around the d'Angelos' Russian olive bushes. He was standing so close I could see the sun-bleached hairs on his arm and the pulse throbbing in his neck and smell the sweet, salty odor of his suntan lotion. It made me dizzy. I wanted to shut my eyes and lean my head against his shoulder.

We both gazed down at the bay.

The *Isle of Fire* sat at the dock, engines humming, while Carl Hayes boarded, followed by his wife, pushing her child in the stroller, and then the Peabodys, my next-door neighbors. As the ferry backed into the channel, seventeen-year-old Sonny Peabody waved goodbye to his parents and walked off the dock to his mother's big blue tricycle, parked by the bicycle rack. (Sonny's mother, like Sharon Jessup and Paula Wohlens, never learned to ride a bicycle. They get around on expensive, adult-sized three wheelers.)

Sonny settled his two hundred and fifty pounds on the saddle of the trike and pedaled slowly up Blueberry. He was wearing shorts and a tee shirt and smiling a fat-cherub smile, and he looked, I thought, like a giant child riding a giant tricycle.

We moved off the walk to let him pass.

"Lily." Will rubbed his chin. "I don't—" He glanced

down Center toward his house and muttered, "Never mind."

Feeling awkward and vaguely guilty, I watched Caroline hurrying toward us. She carried an empty bucket in each hand, but she wasn't going clamming, for she'd changed out of her bathing suit and put on jeans. She wore, in addition, a bright red shirt and a very strange expression—guarded and jumpy and kind of wild, I thought. To my relief, she ignored me.

"Will! Thank goodness you're here. I want you to go for the clams right now."

"Now? I told you I'd get them this afternoon. You didn't have to come running after me," he added irritably. "What the hell's the matter with you?"

I should have walked on and let them argue in private, but the dog took that moment to squat in the sand under the Russian olive bushes.

"Get the clams now," Caroline insisted. "Here." She tried to hand him the buckets. "Take these."

"I will not!" he snapped. "I'll mosey on home and drop off my beach stuff and maybe," he drawled, his voice thick with anger, "maybe I'll have a drink. Then I'll go for your goddamn clams!"

"Oh," she gasped, "but that's too late!" She set the buckets on the walk and stared at them. When she raised her head, she said, "I'm sorry" in a low, contrite voice. "I didn't mean to come on so bossy. It's just that it's almost four, and finding all those clams might take you a long time. I was standing on the corner of the deck, and I saw you down here, and I thought you'd like it if I brought the buckets. I didn't mean to get you angry."

Will stared out at the bay while he calmed down. Then he sighed and said, "Okay, Caroline, don't worry about it. I know you've been upset," he added, as much for my benefit as hers. He gave her his beach things, picked up the buckets, and nodded to me. "See you around."

When I arrived at the courts, Cissy Fry was warming up against Paula and Sharon. "Hurry up!" she called. "I don't like to do this alone!"

On the adjoining court, another lopsided bout of rallying was going on. June Milgrim, in an elegant white knit tennis dress that showed off every curve of her elegant body, was hitting as well as she could against Karen Rosen and a young woman I didn't know, both of whom played as badly as June did. The teaching court was empty. Scotty sprawled on the covered bench, reading a paperback. I sat down next to him and put on my sneakers.

June walked over to the bench. "Scotty, are you busy now?"

"Yes, I am. I have a four o'clock lesson. If he shows." He returned to his book.

I went out on the court with Cissy and warmed up. Then Paula served, and lost, a long, hot first game. We changed sides, and while Cissy took some practice serves, I stood by the bench and mopped my face.

June came off the court again. "Look here, Scotty. Fredericka Borg was supposed to be our fourth, but she cut her foot on a shell at the beach. I need you for a partner. Play with us," she said imperiously.

He flushed and answered her roughly. "I told you I have a lesson."

"Play with us, Scotty," she commanded again, "until your lesson gets here." And she walked back on the court. When he didn't follow her, she turned and asked, "Are you coming?"

"I sure am!" He grabbed his racquet and ball cage and strode angrily to the baseline beside her. "Okay, girls." He shouted across the net as though they were deaf. "Let's warm up!" He hit a slow ball to Karen, but she had to run for it, and when she managed to return it, he shouted, "Good!" and sent it to her backhand. She swung at it five seconds late. Without a pause, he fed her another ball, which she ran for and missed, breathing hard from the effort and the heat, and then another and another. "Getting tired?" he mocked. "I'll warm up your guest. What's her name?"

June said something I couldn't hear in a fierce, low voice.

"Okay, Sylvie," Scotty shouted. "Your turn?"

Cissy, from the baseline on our court, said, "Lily! Whenever you're ready."

"Oh, sorry." I moved up to the net.

Cissy and I won our game—but only because Paula Wohlens ran out of steam faster than I did. When it was over, we both dragged off the court. I collapsed on the bench; Paula filled an empty tennis ball can with water from the fountain and dumped it over her head.

"That's better." She pushed her wet brown bangs off her forehead. "I'm finished. I couldn't chase another tennis ball if my life depended on it."

"It's too hot for tennis." I wiped my face and fanned it with the towel. "Even the wind doesn't help." The afternoon wind, unfailing, had begun to blow.

Karen Rosen conferred at the net with her guest and announced, "We can't play anymore. We're going home."

Scotty grinned. "Why, that's too bad." He watched them leave. I made room on the bench for June, who gave me a small, tired smile.

"Sharon," I called. "Paula and I are quitting. You can play singles with Cissy."

"Not in this heat." Sharon strode off the court, pants flapping around her ankles. She pulled off her tennis hat and fanned herself with it.

"Cover up," I said automatically.

Cissy joined us. "Is it too hot for you?" She put one hand on the part of her anatomy where the rest of us have stomachs, stretched the other straight out at shoulder height, and did a slow demi-plié. "I love the heat. It keeps my muscles warm."

Paula groaned, pulled herself to her feet, and started for the gate. Cissy and Sharon followed her, and a minute later, Scotty collected his balls and left.

June Milgrim, on the bench beside me, said, "Scotty forgot his book," and put it with her balls and racquet to bring home. She smiled shyly. "I'm June Milgrim. My boy Jimmy says that your son . . ." She paused.

"Woody," I filled in.

". . . Woody went off to tennis camp."

"That's right." I pulled off my sneakers and socks.

"I admire you so much for letting him go!"

"I couldn't help myself. He badgered me until I said yes." I tucked the socks into the sneakers and tried to figure out how old she was. She had to be at least twenty-eight or twenty-nine, though she looked younger. Her large green eyes had a soft, sad look about them, the way her son's eyes did.

I glanced at my watch. It told me that today was Saturday, July 2, which I knew already, and four-forty-five, which I didn't know. I was going to have a late dinner alone. Until then, I was free.

"Would you like to come over and have a drink?"

"Oh, yes," she said. "I'd love to."

The Mortimers' pink house sits on a secondary dune four or five feet higher than Paula Wohlens' house, next door, and the Ballou house, across the walk. The front deck looks right at the tennis-court gate. Unless I climbed over the back fence, I had to come out that gate. There was no way to avoid Caroline seeing me—and stopping me and badgering me about her women's group—if she was sitting outside on her deck. She was. I caught a glimpse of her red shirt as I opened the gate, and I looked the other way, directly at June.

"Was your house in good shape when you bought it?"

I asked quickly. "Did it need a lot of work?" For the moment, I hoped it was in shambles; I prayed she would talk and talk. Caroline, even Caroline, wouldn't interrupt two people walking past her house in deep conversation.

"We had most of the work done over the winter," June said and looked past me for an instant, straight at the Mortimer deck. "But I'll tell you, there was sure a lot more to do than we expected."

The new deck, the new kitchen, and the reshingling job on the roof carried us all the way to my house.

I fixed a couple of gin and tonics and a tray of cheese and brought them out to the redwood lounges on my front deck. We sat for a while sipping our drinks and enjoying the ocean—dark blue again, except for a strip of pale green floating on the eastern horizon and a trim of white foam at the shoreline, glistening in the late afternoon sunlight.

"How did you ever find Sharon's Landing?" I asked. "A lot of people who've come to Fire Island for years don't even know about us."

"Through Mr. Fry," she said. "I met him five years ago when Jimmy and I came to New York from Wichita. But I hadn't seen him in years—since my first couple of months in the city—and then I ran into him last summer at the Museum of Modern Art. He remembered my son." She smiled. "When he asked how Jimmy was, and I said just so-so, he started talking about how good Fire Island was for kids. He even told me how to get in touch with the people who rented us their house last August. And then we bought it. Mr. Fry said I'd love it out here, and he was right. I could look at the ocean forever!"

"I could too," I said. "But, you know, my husband always liked the mountains better. What he really wanted was a house on top of a mountain overlooking his own lake. With a waterfall right outside his bedroom window."

"You know what?" Her green eyes sparkled. "I used

to own the house your husband wanted. Almost the very house. Up in the Adirondacks. Only I gave it away."

"You what?"

"It's true!" She was bursting to tell me the whole story. "Three years ago, I had a job as a waitress in a grease joint on Seventh Avenue, when this regular customer I knew hired me for his showroom. Coats and suits. He was divorced. An older man with two married sons. He took to Jimmy right away, and Jimmy just adored him. Jimmy's father died in an oil field accident. That's why we left Wichita. Anyway, when this man and I started going together, the three of us used to spend weekends at his place in the Adirondacks. It had a big fireplace, and the waterfall was down below, just before the stream entered the lake. He was marvelous to Jimmy! When we decided to get married, he made this new will that gave Jimmy a lot of money and me a little money plus the Adirondack house. I signed a paper saying I gave up my right to anything else."

"What happened?"

"A week before we were going to get married, he had a heart attack. At the office. He died just like that! They told me he had two attacks before. I didn't know." She leaned forward and looked at me earnestly. "But his sons claimed that I did, and they tried to break the will. They didn't mind so much about the money, but they hated to lose the house." She sighed. "I didn't want to make trouble, so I said I'd give it back. That satisfied them, and we settled out of court, even though I could have fought it through and won, Leo said. He was my lawyer; we were married right after that, and Leo adopted Jimmy, like he promised." She frowned and looked out at the first fisherman of the evening, casting his line into the ocean beyond the breaking surf.

That should have been the happy ending, I thought, and wondered how long she'd stay married to a man her son hated. And what about Scotty? Did June think she could turn a twenty-one-year-old boy into a father for Jimmy?

It was six-thirty when June left to meet her husband at the ferry. By seven, the wind had changed direction, blowing in heavy, muggy air from the southwest. I rode down to the store, and by the time I rode back, gray clouds shrouded the sky. I put my bike away in the shed, walked the dog, and closed all the windows in the house.

About eight-thirty, it began to drizzle. I put a steak (for one) under the broiler, tossed some lonesome lettuce in my big glass salad bowl, and set a single place on the round oak dining table Henry had overpaid for at a country auction ten years ago.

As I sat down to eat, the drizzle changed to rain. Bo Jessup built our beach houses with roofs, but no ceilings; light rain sounded like marbles bouncing on the shingles, heavy rain like machine-gun fire. The machine guns held off, but just as I finished loading the dishwasher, the clouds above the restless ocean grew thick and black, and the light died suddenly. I switched on the kitchen spots and walked around the living room turning on all the lamps. Outside, in the dark, the surf roared and raged, and the wind picked up, whistling through the telephone wires, sending damp drafts through the cracks under the eaves. Thunder rumbled in the distance. Now I'm in for it, I thought, feeling my stomach knot.

Actually, I almost enjoy a thunderstorm, if I'm watching the fireworks from inside my apartment in a steel-and-concrete skyscraper in New York City. But not on Fire Island, where my shelter is a flimsy beach house perched on skinny locust posts—as bare and exposed on its sand dune as a single pine tree in the middle of a prairie.

I took out emergency supplies—candles, matches, brandy, and a crystal brandy glass—one of a pair remaining from a set of six, a wedding present.

The thunderstorm, rolling in across the bay, announced its approach with a crash so loud it rocked the house. Mops, startled out of his sleep, jumped down from Henry's big chair whimpering with fright. The lights flickered and went out. I managed to light a candle on the third try and fill the glass with brandy without spilling too much on the table. I drank it in great gulps between claps of thunder, while the wind beat against the house and rain hammered on the roof, and lightning flashed through the windows to the west and south.

Then the storm passed overhead. Volleys of thunder shook the house, and lightning blazed through all the windows at once—so close I could hear it sizzle and crack. I covered my ears and shut my eyes tight and put my head down on the table—knocking over the brandy glass; it shattered on the floor. Mops, who was pressing his shaking body against my legs and howling, howled louder. I picked him up and put him on my lap and patted him and talked to him—until the storm moved out over the ocean where fingers of lightning dropped through black clouds and touched the waves. Thunder, muted now, blended with the roar of the surf. The wind grew calm, and the rain changed back to a drizzle.

It's all over, I thought. I'm safe now. I stood up carefully, mindful of my stiff body, found the broom, and swept up the glass by the shadowy light of the candle. I'm safe now, I told myself again, trying to wipe out a budding headache and the flutter of anxiety in my stomach. The storm's gone. There's nothing to be afraid of.

At nine-thirty by my watch, the lights in my living room went on again. The electric clock over the stove had stopped at nine. I reset it, took down the dog's leash, and put on a slicker, which, it turned out, I didn't need. The drizzle had stopped; I stepped outside into a thick, gray fog.

The lights were on again at the Milgrims', and at the Peabodys', where I caught a glimpse of Sonny Peabody lumbering into the kitchen, as I led the dog down the ramp. But at the Huffs' house, on the corner of Holly, only a candle glowed dimly in the kitchen. I decided to look in on Katie Huff's grandmother.

I pushed through the door without knocking.

The old lady sat at the kitchen table in her nightgown and robe, head bowed, hands folded in her lap.

"Matilda! Are you all right?"

She raised her head with its mass of white, wavy hair. "Oh, Lily, my dear. I'm so glad to see you." She spoke in the clipped accent of her native London, but her voice wavered. "The storm frightened me." She lifted a trembling hand to her throat.

I found a bottle of her son's brandy and poured her some, which steadied her. And then her lights went on. "There!" She smiled, showing the small, even teeth of her dentures. "I'm quite all right, now. I don't know why the storm upset me so. Perhaps because I was alone. Katie went to baby-sit at the Girards'. I was tired too," she admitted. "I fixed supper for Katie and Sonny Peabody and played a game of chess with Sonny. And this afternoon, I went for a swim in that lovely ocean!"

I helped her back to bed and brought her a glass of water for her dentures, and sat in her room until her eyes closed, and she began to snore lightly. Then Mops and I went home.

4

I WAS ABOUT to undress and close up for the night when I heard the door to the bicycle shed banging. I grabbed a flashlight out of the kitchen drawer and the shed key off a hook on the pegboard and went outside and around to the ramp that led to the beach stairs. My bicycle shed was under the house, down a short wood walk off the beach-stair ramp. But before I went to work on the shed door, I stood for a moment at the top of the stairs, peering into the dark, thick fog below that swallowed up the bottom half of the stairs and the beach and the ocean beyond it.

The wood railing trembled under my hand; someone was climbing the stairs—quickly and confidently. Some-one local, since he—or she—paused in the middle where the two broken steps were. I didn't wait to see who. I was tired, and I had to deal with the shed door, which was warped and hard to lock. Though it locked on my first try this time. I leaned against it in relief and watched to see who was coming off the beach at ten-thirty at night in this rotten weather.

I turned my flashlight on Caroline Mortimer.

She stopped on the top step, opened a wide-mouth glass jar, and drank from it, long and deep.

I ducked under the corner of the house and walked up the ramp.

"What's in that jar?" I said sharply.

She stopped drinking and wiped her lips on the sleeve of her work shirt, coughing a little.

"Why, martinis, Lily. Just martinis." Holding the jar in both hands, she sat down carefully on the top step. "Homemade. I brought them to my women's group tonight, but nobody drank them. Everybody had white wine. Though they ate all the stuffed clams I made." She leaned back against the first railing post.

"Give me that jar." I held out my hand.

She shook her head. "You'd just pour it out. Right, Lily? No use wasting good liquor." She raised the jar to her lips and drank and drank until it was empty, and then she threw it down the stairs into the fog.

She spit and began to cough. She coughed a long time, motioning me away when I tried to help. She stopped, finally, and put her head in her hands. "I'm sick," she moaned. "Everything's going round and round."

"Come on, Caroline," I sighed. "I'll take you home."

We made it all the way down Beach Plum to her house, and then she vomited into the sand by the ramp. I held her arm and comforted her, and she rewarded me by wiping her mouth on my sleeve and collapsing against the railing.

I couldn't budge her. I was trying to figure out what to do when Will came out of the house. The two of us pulled her to her feet and managed to walk her inside and down the hall to their bedroom. We dropped her on one of their twin beds and she began to snore, her mouth slack, her face smeared with lipstick and vomit.

Will went into the bathroom and came back with a towel and a wet washcloth. "She'll be all right," he said and cleaned her face and patted it dry. "She'll sleep it off." He covered her with the spread from the other bed.

She curled up and pulled the spread under her chin.

"You ought to bury that mess right now, Will," I said.

He left, and I heard him banging around in the storage area on the deck where he kept his tools and his wagon and extra hose for the yard.

After a while, he stuck his head in the door of the bedroom, where I was sitting, watching Caroline sleep.

"It's eleven-thirty," he said, "and it's drizzling again. I'll take you back to your house as soon as I clean off the shovel."

We walked up Blueberry in silence under Will's big black British umbrella. At the foot of my ramp he closed it, and I said, "How about a cup of coffee?"

He smiled. "I thought you'd never ask."

He followed me up the ramp and into the kitchen and seated himself at the round oak table.

I ground the beans and plugged in the pot. "What happened with your daughter?" I asked.

"I'm not sure I know." He tried to smile. "Scotty was Millie's boyfriend last summer. They broke up the middle of August, and she moped around, the way kids do. But she seemed fine again the Monday morning before the Labor Day weekend when I drove her back to the city. She was starting college in a week or so, and I thought she was looking forward to it. Even though Penn wasn't her first choice." He moved around uneasily in his chair. "She wanted a small college." His mouth worked, and his forefinger traced an old scar on the table top. "Anyway, we had a pleasant ride into the city, and I let her off at Bloomingdale's. That was the last we saw of her."

I gasped.

"Oh, she's alive and well; she just left us," he said grimly. "She drew her money out of the bank and caught a plane to California. She called me a week later; it was a pretty awful week." He wiped his mouth with the back of his hand. "She doesn't want me to know where she's living, or how, or with whom. But she keeps in touch, and that's a good sign. She phones a couple of times a month, and she's written twice. To me. At the office. She refuses to talk to her mother or write to her. That's really the worst part of it." He looked down at his hands. "Caroline blames the whole thing on Scotty and June Milgrim."

He pushed himself away from the table and stood up and began pacing back and forth between Henry's big chair and the front windows. "Ever since Millie left, Caroline's been drinking too much. And she refuses to get help—to go to AA, or a psychiatrist, or even to talk about it to a friend. I don't know what I'm going to do."

The coffee was ready and I filled two mugs.

"Well," I said, bringing the mugs to the table, "why don't you have some coffee? It can't hurt."

He turned and smiled at me, and I lost my head, I guess, for I smiled back with all my cockles showing. He put one hand on my shoulder; with the other, he switched off the light and pulled me to him. Then he kissed me on the lips and on the neck just above the collarbone—and a lot of other places, after a while, after we shooed the dog out of the bedroom and closed the door behind him, and carefully removed each other's clothes.

In the middle of the night, Will went home to check on Caroline. He promised to come back, but I was afraid he couldn't, and I worried about it—while I showered and walked the dog and fixed a tray of Brie and crackers and grapes—until I heard him climb the ramp and cross the deck to the kitchen door.

"I woke her," he said. "She paid a visit to the bathroom and changed into a nightgown, complaining all the time about her headache, and went right back to sleep. I took the phone off the hook, just in case my service called." Then he grinned. "And I brought along champagne for us. It's cold. I took it out of the refrigerator."

He opened it and poured us some to drink with our food, and then one thing led to another, and I didn't think about Caroline again until after we finished off the champagne, sitting up in bed against a pile of pillows, sipping slowly from the same glass, and listening to the ocean roar and the wind whistle through the telephone wires.

He's ready to leave her, I told myself, so I should stop feeling guilty. Then he turned off the light and invited me to sleep in the crook of his arm.

III
Sunday, July 3

5

I WOKE JUST before dawn, rested and full of beans. Will stood in the gray half-light by the window, buttoning his work shirt and tucking it into his jeans. I invited him to stick around a little longer.

He leaned down and kissed me and said, "No. It's already too late. Somebody might see me walking home. In these clothes too! I should be wearing swim trunks; I'm usually jogging on the beach by now."

"Want to go for a jog? I'll find you something you can wear.

I gave him a tan bathing suit of Henry's, a plain white tee shirt, and a white towel. He changed; I pulled on shorts, a tennis shirt, and an old gray sweatshirt, and we came out on the deck. Will vaulted the deck railing and climbed down the dune stairs. He was hanging the towel and tee shirt on the lifeguard stand when the sun came up, lighting the pale, cloudless sky and the empty white beach. He waved and gave me a glorious smile. As he turned and started for the hard-packed sand at the shoreline, I looked out at the high, white surf shimmering in the sunlight, so that both of us in almost the same instant saw the log bobbing behind the first row of breakers. Only it wasn't a log.

Will ran to the water and plunged in. Diving through a cresting wave, he swam to the dark shape and, seizing it by a leg, floated it over the top of the breakers. Then he picked it up and carried it to shore. Just beyond the reach of the tide, he eased his burden on to the sand and examined it, his back to me, blocking my view.

Suddenly I remembered how to move. I raced across the deck and down to the beach, grabbing Will's towel and tee shirt as I passed the lifeguard stand.

"Stop!" he commanded.

I stopped, and he walked over to me. He took the towel and tee shirt and used them to cover the face and trunk and part of the legs. I could still see that hair—that familiar, copper-colored hair—tangled, stiff with salt water, trailing strands of seaweed.

"The police! Shall I call them?"

"Yes. No, never mind." His voice was strained and weary. "The squad car that goes up to Ocean Beach should be along any minute. It passes me every morning when I jog."

I stared at the bloated feet, bleached white by the ocean, dense and cold as marble. Moving closer, I gaped at the grotesque bulge of the stomach under the towel. "Oh God," I breathed, nausea rising in my throat.

"Are you okay?" Will asked.

I wasn't but I nodded anyway. "Can you tell when it happened?"

"Last night. Maybe early this morning. They used to wash up within a few hours, but the currents have been strange ever since Ocean Beach built those jetties and blocked the littoral drift." He stared out over the water, his mouth tightening into a grim line. "And it didn't just happen, Lily. Somebody helped it along. Somebody shot our friend here. In the chest, below the shoulder. And then left him to drown."

"Who?" I gasped. "Who could have done that?"

Panic flared in his eyes. He looked away, down the beach. A blue-and-white police station wagon, its headlights on, plowed slowly through the deep sand half a mile to the west.

"I know a policeman out here," I said suddenly, "Harry Bell, a friend of my brother George. Harry heads up the homicide department for Suffolk County, and he's a nice man. I had lunch with him and George about three weeks ago. Maybe I ought to call him."

"You know him," Will said. "That can't hurt."

"It may not help, either," I said grimly.

Will dropped to his knees and leaned over the body. When he stood up, I saw he was holding something. His body was still wet; a trickle of water dripped down his leg from his bathing suit, and he shivered as he moved close to me.

"Take them! Quick!"

I took the objects he pressed into my hand and put them in the pocket of my sweatshirt.

"Get rid of them!" he pleaded. "Or Caroline—" He sucked in his breath and moved away from me.

The police car stopped by the lifeguard stand, and two policemen jumped out. The dark-haired one who was driving reached us first. "What happened?" he demanded.

Will lifted the towel and tee shirt and showed him the swollen, twisted body of Scotty Banks.

6

THE TIDE ROARED in, hurling heavy breakers at the beach. Seating himself in the station wagon, the dark-haired policeman rolled up the windows to shut out the racket and called headquarters. Will and I, waiting with his partner beside the body, watched him through the windshield. His lips moved soundlessly. He paused, frowning at the dashboard, and wrote in his notebook, resting it on the rim of the steering wheel. Then he spoke again. I read his lips as they formed Scotty's name.

When the policeman had finished his call, he and his partner pounded stakes into the sand and strung the stakes with rope, surrounding the body, sealing it off for the homicide people. I forced myself to look at Scotty once more, to see him in my mind the moment before the bullet entered his chest—and the moment after. I pictured him sprawled in the shallow water, bleeding, unconscious, left to drown by the man or woman who shot him. By his murderer, I corrected myself, shaking with rage. When the shaking stopped, I found I was weeping, but my stomach settled, and my head began to work. I dried my eyes on my sweatshirt sleeve and thought about the things in my pocket. I had to know what they were. I had to get off the beach.

Will, rubbing his arms and shivering, gave me a reason to leave. "Lily, do you have a jacket at your place I could borrow?"

I said, "I'll find something." Pointing out my house to the policemen, I told them I'd be back in five minutes and walked off the beach as quickly as I dared. Crossing my deck, I hurried into the kitchen through the sliding glass door and emptied the objects onto the counter by the toaster. I knew at once that they belonged to someone in Sharon's Landing. But I couldn't tell who—and I was almost certain the police couldn't tell either. One was a piece of blue cloth, wet, wrinkled, gritty with sand—a pocket flap off a cotton work shirt. The kind people wore on every beach I'd ever been to—from Fire Island to Mikonos. An ordinary metal key chain ran through a buttonhole in the pocket flap and through a hole in the other object: a red hard-plastic tag about two inches long with "Sharon's Landing Property Owners' Association" printed on one side. It must have been panic that made Will hide that tag, for nothing, nothing at all, connected it specifically to Caroline or anyone else. There were forty red tags floating around the community, and all of them were identical.

I allowed myself a small sigh of relief. Caroline was still in trouble; she had threatened Scotty in front of a dozen witnesses. But the objects on my countertop didn't implicate her, and that solved one of my problems. I didn't need to get rid of the things.

I walked to the glass door and peered down at the beach. Will, his back to the two policemen, stared up at my house wondering, no doubt, what was taking me so long, and worrying about Caroline. I wasted the next couple of minutes feeling jealous and put-upon and wishing (with part of me) that Will wasn't quite such a good, kind, responsible man. No matter how much I meant to him, he'd never leave his wife, I knew, as long as the police, or anyone else, suspected her of murder! Then I pulled myself together, walked back to the kitchen counter, and considered, as carefully as I could, how to get Caroline Mortimer out of the mess she was in.

To begin with, I didn't think she killed Scotty. It's one

thing to say "I could kill him" or "I could kill him for that," and quite another to go out and shoot him in cold blood because he split up, ten months ago, with her seventeen-year-old daughter.

The police, however, might not share my opinion—not after they asked around, and people told them what Caroline had said about Scotty. She could be in deep trouble, unless the police turned up the murderer. If they ever did. If they even knew where to start looking without the evidence on my countertop.

The kitchen phone, a small, white Princess, hung on the wall above the toaster. I took it off the receiver and tried to talk myself into calling Harry Bell. He was a smart detective, one of the best in the country, according to my brother George. He'd find Scotty's killer if anyone could, especially if I gave him some help. I liked Harry, and he liked me; I'd be able to tell him things I couldn't tell a stranger. And I was sure he'd come out to Sharon's Landing; all I had to do was ask him!

I sighed and bit my lip and finally admitted that I was afraid to ask him. I didn't have the slightest idea what he'd uncover. Who killed Scotty, I wondered grimly, if Caroline hadn't? Which one of my neighbors? Which one of my friends?

I stared through the glass door at the breakers pounding on the beach and at the current, behind them, flowing east to west, rippling dangerously. Then I looked out at Will and thought about the two of us and scraped up some courage—enough to ask the operator to get me Lieutenant Bell at Suffolk County Police Headquarters.

Will was waiting for me at the bottom of the beach stairs. As I handed him Henry's old tennis jacket, he glanced over his shoulder at the two policemen. They couldn't hear him even if he shouted, but he whispered anyway. "What did you do with those things?"

I didn't answer. I didn't need to. When he slipped on the jacket, he felt the objects in the right-hand pocket.

"What the hell?" he stared at me.

"We don't have to get rid of them. They don't implicate Caroline. If anything, they could help to clear her. They're evidence that might lead to the killer. The police ought to see them."

"If they do, I'll visit Caroline in jail."

"No, you won't," I insisted. "Not if she didn't shoot Scotty. Those things could have belonged to a couple of dozen other people in Sharon's Landing. Think about it!"

He thought about it, frowning into the dune, still shivering in spite of the jacket. Behind him, a second police car bumped through the sand, its siren muted by the surf.

"Maybe you're right. It was stupid of me to mess around." He rubbed his hands together nervously. "But what can I do now? I can't put them back, for God's sake!"

"Give them to Harry Bell, the detective I told you about. I called him, and he's coming out here. Tell him you made a mistake. He's a nice man and—"

"Cut it!" Will said sharply. "Company's coming."

The dark-haired policeman walked toward us. "Dr. Mortimer. Could we see you a minute?"

I started to go along and changed my mind. The policemen seemed to have forgotten me. I decided to go home and wait for Harry Bell in comfort, in a lounge chair on my front deck.

I climbed the beach stairs, and when I reached the top I saw I had a visitor—a frightened, seventeen-year-old, two-hundred-and-fifty-pound visitor. Sonny Peabody blocked the entrance to my ramp. The boy was dressed for jogging in gray sweat pants and a peach-colored tee shirt decorated, front and center, with chessmen.

"That's Scotty out there, isn't it?"

I nodded.

"He's dead, isn't he?"

I took his arm and led him up the ramp to my deck.

"Tell me please, Mrs. Lambert," he demanded, his body shaking, knights and pawns quivering on his tee shirt.

"He's dead."

"Oh my God," he moaned. "Oh my God." He collapsed into a chair and put his face in his hands.

I patted his back and waited for him to stop crying. He was a funny kid—shy, quiet, a loner. Though he'd finished his first year at Princeton, he was only seventeen and seemed younger. His main Fire Island activity was sitting. He seldom left his deck except to run errands for his mother on her big three-wheeler.

He raised his head finally. "I'm sorry, Mrs. Lambert, but he was my friend!" He wiped his nose on the back of his hand. "He used to come up on my deck, and we'd talk about things. Like how we didn't get along with our parents and things like that and what we were going to do when we finished college." His voice trailed away, and he looked out at the ocean. After a minute, he asked, "When did it happen?"

"Last night or this morning."

His mouth dropped open, and he looked at me with dismay. "But he was over at my house last night! I can't believe it! He was over at my house!" He shook his head. "It was the first time he'd been over since he moved in with that—with those people." He sniffed and wiped his nose again. "We played chess, and when the storm came and the lights went out, we lit a candle and sat and talked." His eyes filled with tears. "He told me he was sure I could lose weight if I really put my mind to it. I've been fasting all day today! I was going to start jogging this morning, real early, before anybody got up. I set the alarm clock, and when I came outside on the deck, there was Dr. Mortimer coming out of the water with—" He put his fist in front of his mouth.

"How late did you and Scotty talk?"

"Until the lights went back on; then he had to leave. He had a date with Ramona Zarrow." He looked out at the ocean again. "Oh my God! How did it happen?" He was a swimming teacher, for God sakes! How could a swimming teacher drown?"

"Sonny," I said gently, "somebody shot him first."

7

AT SIX A.M. the police helicopter circled the beach and settled on the sand like a huge blue beetle. Two men in civilian clothes climbed out. The older one, my brother's friend, Harry Bell, unbuttoned his plaid sports jacket, stepped over the ropes around the body, and squatted beside it. After a few minutes, he rose and spoke to several of the men in civilian clothes who arrived in a third police car and to Will. Then he buttoned his jacket, straightened his tie, and walked to the beach stairs.

He was a square, muscular man, half a head shorter than Will, who came with him up on my deck. With the sunlight glinting on his silver sideburns, and the wind blowing his dark hair away from the bald spot on the top of his head, he looked older than I had guessed when I met him three weeks before at lunch with him and George—forty-eight, maybe fifty. His face, unexpectedly bony above his compact body, was pleasantly ugly; when he smiled (he had smiled a lot when we had lunch together), wrinkles fanned out from the corners of his hazel eyes.

But he wasn't smiling now, and he didn't greet me by name. "Sorry I'm here on such unpleasant business." He spoke formally, putting space between us, making sure I understood that he had a murder to solve and no favors to give. To guarantee I wouldn't ask for any, he brought along a witness. "One of my detectives is joining us." He motioned toward the blond young man striding up the ramp.

Detective Fred Mulloy shook my hand more gently than I expected, considering the boldness of his flower-patterned tie, the muscles bulging beneath his light summer shirt, and the handgun hanging in a black leather holster on his hip. "Pleased to meet you," he said, and then he came with me into the kitchen and helped carry coffee and sweet rolls out to the side deck.

The four of us sat down on the curved benches around my redwood table. Below us, on the beach, a police photographer snapped pictures of the body. A fourth blue-and-white vehicle joined the others. This one, I saw, was an ambulance.

Harry Bell took a pen and a small loose-leaf notebook from his breast pocket. Clearing his throat, he asked a question he knew the answer to already. "You brought the body out of the water, Dr. Mortimer?"

"Yes." Will warmed his hands around his coffee mug.

"Did you examine it?"

"Enough to see that there was a bullet wound in the chest, on the right-hand side, below the shoulder joint."

"Do you think it killed him?"

"I doubt it," Will said slowly. "Though it probably knocked him unconscious long enough for him to drown. Your people will have to find that out," he added irritably.

"I know." Harry sipped his coffee. "But we won't have the M.E.'s report for a couple of hours. We'll save some time if you can help us. How long was the body in the water, would you guess?"

"Since last night—but that's a very rough guess."

"Is it possible he shot himself?"

"It would have been damned hard. The bullet angled in too close to his right shoulder. And he was right-handed; at least he played tennis with his right hand."

"Any sign of a struggle?"

"A couple of broken fingernails."

"Anything else?"

Will paused and looked out at the water, and I held my breath.

"Yes," he said finally. "Scotty ripped something off his assailant's shirt; it caught on his watchband—one of those heavy metal stretch bands. God knows how, but it stayed there."

Harry raised his eyebrows. "I saw the watchband, but I didn't see anything caught in it."

"You wouldn't have." Will's voice was expressionless. "It came off while I was examining it, and I kept it. I'm sorry. I wasn't thinking." He put his hand in the pocket of Henry's jacket. "Here it is."

He laid the things on the table and smoothed out the pocket flap.

"Torn off a denim work shirt," I offered. "The kind we all wear. I have one."

"I have a couple of them," Will added. "And so does my wife."

"I see." Harry put on a pair of reading glasses and studied the red tag.

"It's an identification tag for the tennis courts," I explained. "We used them one summer, four years ago, when a lot of people tried to play on our courts who weren't supposed to. The beach, I'm sure you know, is public property; anyone can use it. But the tennis courts belong to the twenty families who own houses in Sharon's Landing. Renters are entitled to play, and overnight visitors. But nobody from other communities. Anyway, the tennis committee had the tags made—two for each household—and asked us to bring them down when we played. But the next year, we began a sign-up system and hired Scotty to look after the courts, and since then, nobody's had to bother with the tags. A lot of people probably threw theirs out."

Harry peered at me over the top of his glasses. "Do you still have yours?"

"Yes. I'll get them."

I crossed the deck and went into my kitchen. Opening the catch-all drawer by the stove, I fished among half-used candles, unused house keys, this year's grocery slips, and last year's ferry schedules until I found the red tags; both were attached to metal key chains.

"May I keep them?" Harry asked, and I nodded.

Fred Mulloy, the young detective, asked, "Where was the key chain caught, Dr. Mortimer? Where on the wristband?"

"Inside the arm at about the thumb joint." Will grimaced. "I should have put it back. I'm sorry. I just wasn't thinking."

Harry said, "I understand" rather kindly, I thought. "You'll have to give us a formal statement later on at headquarters. But I'm glad you told us. Some people wouldn't have." He took off his glasses. "Did Scotty have any enemies, Dr. Mortimer? Mrs. Lambert?"

Neither of us said a word.

"Did he have a fight with anyone?" He looked at Will and then at me. "Did anyone have a grudge against him?"

Finally, Will said, "Everyone out here knows my wife hated Scotty."

Harry nodded and waited for him to explain.

"He was my daughter's boyfriend. When they broke up last summer, my daughter ran away from home."

"Why did they break up?"

"I don't know." Will shrugged. "My wife says everything was fine until the Milgrims moved out here last August. My wife thinks Scotty and Mrs. Milgrim were lovers. She blames them both about our daughter."

"Has your daughter returned?"

"No. She's somewhere in California. She won't tell us where—or what she's doing. She phones me at the office every couple of weeks, just to let me know she's okay. I'm thankful for that." He wiped his mouth on the back of his hand. "But she absolutely refuses to talk to her mother. It's had my wife frantic!"

"Frantic? What do you mean?" Harry asked quickly.

"Upset. She's *very* upset. She damn well has a right to be!" he said angrily.

Harry folded his arms across his chest. "How about you, Dr. Mortimer? Do you blame Scotty?"

"I do not," Will said stiffly. "Plenty of seventeen-year-olds break up with their boyfriends without running away. My daughter overreacted. I don't know why. Maybe it's our fault." He rubbed his hands back and forth on his bare thighs.

"Do you know how we can get in touch with Scotty's family?"

Will shook his head. "No, I'm sorry. I think he came from Albany."

"The Milgrims probably have his address," I offered. "He boarded with them out here. That is, Mrs. Milgrim paid him to stay at their house as a kind of companion for her young son."

Harry raised his eyebrows. "How did Mr. Milgrim like that?"

"Not very much. I'd talk to him if I were you. And maybe you better talk to his wife about the argument she and Scotty had on the tennis court yesterday afternoon. She didn't take it seriously. But Scotty did. He was furious!"

"Anyone else we ought to see, Mrs. Lambert?"

I realized I was busy trying to put suspicion on anyone but Caroline. But I was just pointing Harry at possibilities. He could find his own way to certainty.

"Carl Hayes—a nasty character who rents a house

right across from Dr. Mortimer. I think he had a grudge against Scotty." I described the argument about the baby-sitter and added, "But Carl Hayes doesn't seem to like *anyone* out here!"

Will said, "If you don't need me for a while, I'd like to go home and take a shower." After he gave Harry his phone number, he walked across the deck and down the ramp. Then he came back. "They're awake at the Milgrims'. I saw the housekeeper moving around in the kitchen. I know you're anxious to talk to them."

Harry closed his notebook. "Want to come along?" he asked me. "It would make things easier if you introduced us and broke the news about Scotty."

I followed him onto the front deck. The body on the beach was gone, carried off, I assumed, by the ambulance now weaving west through the sand. Harry and Fred Mulloy went down the beach stairs and huddled with the policemen, who had regrouped with their cars at the foot of the dune. I waited by the ramp, watching the helicopter spin its propeller, sputter, and rise in a whirlwind of sand. Sunlight burned through the last trace of fog on the ocean, and a fisherman cast his line into the same patch of water where I first saw the body.

8

THE MILGRIMS' HOUSEKEEPER, a small, cinnamon-skinned woman in her mid-sixties, stood in the doorway and watched us climb the ramp.

"This is Lieutenant Bell," I said, "and Detective Mulloy. May we come in? It's about Scotty."

She nodded, her eyes wide with fear. "He didn't come home last night. I was so worried."

"He's dead, Esmée."

"Dead!" She gasped and began to tremble.

Harry Bell took her arm and led her to a chair by the kitchen table. "Fred. Get some water."

The young detective filled a glass at the kitchen tap. Esmée drank a little, said "Thank you" in a choked voice, and stopped shaking. "How . . . ?"

"He drowned in the ocean," Harry told her. "But somebody shot him first."

"Oh, no," she moaned. Her body stiffened; she squeezed her eyes shut and began to rock back and forth, grieving, I thought, for some other man who died violently. Someone who meant a lot more to her than Scotty did.

I stood around by the doorway feeling like a pariah, while Fred Mulloy filled her glass again and Harry sat with her at the table and said, "Feeling better now?" when she stopped rocking and opened her eyes and sipped the water.

She nodded. Ignoring me, she smiled gratefully at the two of them. Then she frowned and began to worry about Jimmy Milgrim.

"Poor child! He loved Scotty so. It will be terrible for him. He's such a sensitive boy!" The words rolled on her tongue, their cadence Jamaican, I guessed, or Bermudan. "Is he still sleeping?" I asked.

She shook her head. "He slept at the d'Angelos' and Mr. d'Angelo took him fishing with the twins this morning. He loves to fish." She wiped her eyes with the corner of her apron. "Poor boy."

She meant Jimmy, of course.

I nodded. "He's going to take it awfully hard. Is Mrs. Milgrim awake yet?"

"Mrs. Milgrim, she left on a seaplane with Mr. Milgrim early, early, when the sun came up. Mr. Milgrim had business in the city. Missus, she went to the airport to see her brother for two hours. He's a sergeant in the army, flying off to Germany. She be back this morning."

I frowned. "Taki Andreapolis ought to be the one to tell Jimmy about Scotty. He's a child psychiatrist, a really fine one," I explained. "I'll talk to him as soon as I can. I know he'll be glad to help."

"Good." Harry pulled on a sideburn and turned to Esmée. "Do you have Scotty's home address or phone number?"

She shook her head. "Maybe when Mrs. Milgrim . . ."

"We really shouldn't wait that long." He smiled at her, his eyes crinkling at the corners. "If you take us to Scotty's room, maybe we can find a letter from his parents or an address book."

She led us to a small jewel of a bedroom in the back of the house, furnished by June Milgrim, or her decorator, with navy blue shutters at the casement windows, a navy down comforter on the bed, a yellow rug on the floor and a trio of Miró prints splashing red and blue and yellow on the white walls. Scotty had kept it as bare and impersonal as an unoccupied hotel room. I wondered why, and then I figured out that he must have felt uncomfortable living with the Milgrims. Not a single object of his was in sight. Even his tennis gear was invisible, stowed neatly in the closet, which Fred Mulloy, the young detective, opened briefly. A bright red electric clock, running thirty minutes late, sat on the white formica table by the bed. Harry glanced at it, and then opened the top drawer of the white formica chest of drawers. He removed a letter and an address book which he thumbed through quickly after putting on his glasses.

"This'll do." He wrote some names and numbers in his notebook and put the letter and address book back.

I followed them into the kitchen. When they sat down at the table again, Harry asked Esmée to tell him every-thing she remembered about the last time she had seen Scotty.

She leaned back in her chair and folded her hands in her lap over her small, neat apron. "Only last night. I gave him his supper with the little boys—Jimmy and the d'Angelo twins. The twins had dinner here, and then Jimmy went over to their house to spend the night. I fed them early, at six. Steak, it was, with blueberry pie for dessert. Then Scotty thanked me, the way he always did, poor boy, and said, 'See you later, Esmée.' Only I never saw him again." She paused and frowned at something.

"What is it?" Harry prodded.

"I was just thinking that he came back after that, even though I didn't see him. Because the brownies were gone. He asked me at supper if I could make him some to take to a party he was going to. He said he'd be back to get them around nine. I baked them right away and let them cool while I served Mr. and Mrs. Milgrim their dinner. I frosted them after I cleaned up and left them on the table in a cardboard box and went back to my room with my friend from Dunewood who came for a visit."

"What time was that?"

"About a quarter to nine. Just before the thunder and lightning. It was a terrible storm! The lights went out at nine o'clock. They usually do; we keep candles in the kitchen, and when I took one out of the drawer and lit it, I noticed that the brownies were still there. But later, when I let my friend out the kitchen door, the box of brownies was gone. That's how I knew he came back."

Harry leaned forward, his elbows on the table. "Do you remember what time your friend left?"

"Ten-thirty."

"Exactly?" He raised his eyebrows.

"Yes. I looked at my watch to reset the clock on the electric stove."

"Could somebody else have taken the brownies?" I asked. "Mr. or Mrs. Milgrim? Or Jimmy and the twins?"

She shook her head. "They never eat sweets, those two." She nodded toward the stairs on the other side of the living room. "Jimmy and the twins were already at the d'Angelos'."

"Did Mrs. Milgrim leave the house during the evening?" Harry asked. "Or Mr. Milgrim?"

"I don't know. My room is in the back, and my friend and I were talking. Their bedroom and Mr. Milgrim's study are upstairs. I don't hear them come or go."

Harry pulled on one of his sideburns. "You and Mrs. Milgrim and Jimmy have already moved out here for the summer. Am I right?"

She nodded. "Three weeks ago."

"Scotty moved in with you at the same time?"

"Yes."

"Mr. Milgrim usually spends his weekends at Fire Island, but he stays in the city during the week. Is that correct?"

She stiffened and said coldly, "If you have any more questions, I'm sure Mrs. Milgrim will answer them."

She rose and showed us to the door.

9

THE THREE OF us left the Milgrim house, though not
exactly together. I trailed down the ramp after the two
men, staring at the back of Harry's jacket and the thin,
dark hair at the nape of his neck. I thought he'd forgotten
me completely, but when we crossed the walk, he turned
and said, "Thank you for coming with us" politely
enough, but as wary and distant as the moment he
stepped on my deck, an hour before. "Wait here. I'll be
right back," he added and disappeared with Fred Mulloy
down the steps to the beach.

I waited. I leaned on the railing to the stairs and dug a
hole with my heel in a damp patch of sand. What good
did it do, I asked myself bitterly, to have a friend on the
case if he didn't act friendly? How could I help find a
murderer the way I had planned if my friend the detective treated me like one of the suspects?

Harry appeared on the steps alone, frowning, with-
drawn. "Let's have a talk," he said brusquely and motioned toward my ramp. We climbed in silence, and he
walked me to the redwood lounges in the center of my
deck—the one place where Fred Mulloy and the policemen on the beach below could see us, but couldn't hear
us.

Then he addressed me by my first name for the first
time all morning. "Sit down, Lily."

I sat down; he didn't. He leaned his backside against
the deck railing and crossed his arms over his chest. "I
want straight answers. Do you understand?"

I nodded, licking my lips. I intended to tell him the straight truth—but maybe not the whole truth.

"Who killed Scotty?" he asked.

"I don't have the slightest idea. Only that it must have been someone from Sharon's Landing. I told you that when I called," I added irritably.

"What made you so sure the killer wasn't an outsider?"

"The tennis tag and the flap from the work-shirt pocket. I'd seen the combination before. A lot of people put their tags on key chains and looped them through the butotnhole on their work-shirt pocket. I did; my husband did. Paula and John Wohlens, Cissy Fry. Oh, I can't remember everybody!"

"The Mortimers?" he asked pointedly.

"Probably. Well, yes," I admitted. "It was a convenient way to carry the tag down to the courts; it never got lost, and it didn't have to be taken off when the shirt went through the wash." I cleared my throat and added, "Is this answer straight enough, or am I twisting and turning too much?"

"Go on." His face was expressionless.

"Most of us who own houses out here only used the tags one summer, four years ago. I took ours off the following spring and put them away in a kitchen drawer. I don't know what other people did; I never even gave it a thought until this morning, when I realized that one person, at least, never bothered to remove the tag. He—or she—must have tucked it into the pocket, buttoned the flap, and forgot about it. Only a couple of the links on the key chain would have showed when the shirt was worn. We wear our work shirts forever out here. The older and more faded they are, the better we like them."

"Was there anything else to make you think that someone from Sharon's Landing was the killer?"

"No. Nothing."

"Then you saw the objects before you phoned me?"

I nodded.

"When they were still caught in the victim's watch-band?"

I shook my head.

"Then Dr. Mortimer showed them to you?"

"Not exactly."

"Come, come, Lily," he said harshly. "You can do better than that."

"You're right. I guess I can." I sighed and sat up straight and pulled in my stomach and said, "Will gave them to me just as the police arrived. I hid them in my sweatshirt pocket."

"You *hid* them?" His face turned gray.

I squeezed my hands together and kept going.

"I didn't know what they were until five or ten minutes later when I looked at them in my kitchen. Will thought they implicated his wife—I don't know why. He wanted me to get rid of them, but I talked him out of the idea. I persuaded him to give the things to you."

He ignored my explanation. "Why, I ought to arrest the two of you for tampering with evidence!"

"But you got your evidence back. Isn't that enough? Doesn't that make up for Will's mistake? And mine? Some people wouldn't have bothered to give the things back. If I tossed them in the garbage, you wouldn't even know they existed—and I wouldn't have all this trouble."

I must have sounded belligerent, but I was worried. Will's panicky action could make things worse instead of better, by calling Harry's attention to Caroline.

"You ought to be grateful to me," I added.

"Grateful!" he snapped angrily. But he didn't say another word about arresting us. Not then, anyway. Instead, he changed the subject, more or less.

"Why did you phone me, Lily?"

74

"Because when we had lunch with George, you told me to call if I ever needed you."

"You must have known someone from my office would be out here. There's no homicide squad on the island."

"I wanted *you* to come out—not just anybody from homicide! I couldn't talk to a stranger."

"You would have had to," he said icily. "But what's *your* interest? Why is it so important to you?"

"What do you mean?" I said angrily. "A young man— almost a boy—I knew and liked is murdered. Wouldn't I . . ."

"Lily."

"It's a private matter," I said sulkily.

He didn't like my answer.

"I wish you'd take my word for it," I pleaded.

"Nothing's private in a murder case."

"Do I have to tell you?"

"I'm afraid you do." He waited.

"The fact is"—I swallowed cautiously— "the fact is, I'm thinking seriously about walking off with another woman's husband. Caroline Mortimer's husband, to be exact."

To my surprise, that bothered him. He stiffened and looked away. "Go on."

"It's a shaky marriage, of course. You understand that," I insisted, feeling guilty and defensive. "Will isn't happy with her." I frowned. "Anyway, up until this morning, things looked promising for the two of us. But he won't leave her now, not until you find out who the murderer is."

"Why not?"

I had to say it. "Because Caroline Mortimer could be a . . . could be one suspect. And as long as she's under suspicion, as long as anyone has the slightest doubt about her innocence, Will's going to stay with her. He's that kind of man. He's loyal and good, and he spends every day of his life helping people who are in trouble. And he's never forgotten how much he owes his wife. She was a teacher; she put him through medical school."

"What happens if our investigation doesn't turn out the way you want it to? If Mrs. Mortimer's the killer?"

"Then I'll know where I stand, won't I? It can't be any worse for me than having her a suspect in an unsolved murder. Besides, I don't think for a minute that Caroline killed Scotty. She'd have to keep it a secret, and that's not her style. She copes with her troubles by telling them to everybody who'll listen. Of course," I hedged, "I could be wrong."

Harry unfolded his arms and pulled on a sideburn. "I wonder," he murmured.

He was thinking now, instead of raging, which gave me a chance to say, "You know," (as if it had just occurred to me), "it would make your job a lot easier if you had someone from Sharon's Landing tell you all about the people out here and how the place functions. There aren't any street numbers or names on the houses, so you need a local guide just to show you who lives where. If you want me to, I could draw you a map. And fill you in on everyone. Most of the men in Sharon's Landing and half the women come out to Fire Island only for the weekend. If you haven't solved your murder by tomorrow night, by the time the last ferry leaves, you'll be tracking down people all over the city and out in Westchester and New Jersey and Pennsylvania—four and a half hours into Pennsylvania, where John Wohlens is acting president at some little college!"

Harry scowled at me and at the tips of his loafers and at the two-by-four cedar deck boards and back at me again. "I don't have much choice, do I?"

"You won't be sorry," I said quickly.

"I damn well better not be!" he snapped. "At least

you've been honest with me, Lily, and I appreciate that. But I don't condone your hiding that tennis tag, and I want you to know it." His eyes narrowed. "And if you let me down, I'll run you into headquarters faster than you can blink, and slap a charge on you for tampering. You *and* your friend Dr. Mortimer," he added harshly.

He leaned over the railing, caught Fred Mulloy's attention, and motioned to him to come up on the deck. Then he opened his notebook, took out two sheets of paper, and handed them to me with a pencil from his inside pocket.

"Now draw that map, if you please."

I sketched quickly, using one sheet of paper for the fourteen houses on the ocean side of Center Walk and another sheet for the structures on the bay side: the three tennis courts, the fire shed behind the courts, a parking lot for wagons down by the dock, and the remaining six houses.

"I've put the owners' names on each house and the renters, or other occupants, in parentheses. And I've noted the color of the house. The builder, Bo Jessup, covered each house with special siding in a pastel color, to make the community look like Bermuda. Bo spent his honeymoon in Bermuda."

I gave the map to Harry, who studied it for a moment and then clipped it in his notebook. "Now tell me about Scotty. What was he like?"

I thought a minute and said, "Warm and friendly with everyone. Responsible; you could always count on him. He enjoyed his work and all the people out here. A bright kid—a promising scholar, in fact, according to Paula Wohlens. She helped him get a fellowship for graduate work next fall. Too bad," I murmured, my control almost slipping away. "He was a good tennis player, but he thought he should be better, and he swore at himself after every poor shot. Though I never heard him swear off the court, until Saturday morning when he had that argument with Carl Hayes. He was absolutely wonderful with kids, and they idolized him. A very nice young man, I'd say."

Harry made a note for himself, and then turned back to the map. "This is the first case I've ever had with forty suspects!"

"Forty?"

He smiled at me for the first time all morning. "One for each of the tennis tags. Is there a master list of everybody out here? We need phone numbers. And city addresses—just in case we *don't* find the murderer by the last ferry tomorrow."

"Cissy Fry has a list. She's secretary of the property owners' association." I looked at my watch. "I'm supposed to play tennis with her at eight."

"Go ahead. I have plenty to do for the next hour. Tell Mrs. Fry we'll be over for her list around nine-thirty. And, Lily, would you mind if we set up field headquarters in your living room? Your house is in a good spot for us." He nodded toward the beach stairs. "I'll station my sergeant here and bring in a couple of telephone lines."

"That's fine with me," I said. "There's a card table in the hall closet for your phones."

He consulted the map. "After your game, look for me at the blue house on the corner across the walk from the courts. We'll have a talk with Carl Hayes."

He was in no hurry, I noticed, to see Caroline Mortimer. Neither was I, for that matter.

"Something on your mind?" Harry asked.

"No. Well, yes there is. The Mortimers' daughter. Someone should tell her—Scotty was her friend. But we don't know how to reach her. Can you ask the police in California to look for her?

"We already asked them." He smiled again, wrinkles fanning out from the corners of his eyes. "I don't think they'll have to look too hard. I found a letter from Millie Mortimer in the drawer in Scotty's bureau; she put her address on the back of the envelope."

10

IT WAS TIME for my tennis date, and I dreaded it. I didn't want to be the one to tell everyone about Scotty. I hoped that somehow the news had spread already, by that mysterious grapevine that operates in small groups like ours. But no such luck. I rode down to the courts and parked my bike in the stands next to Sharon Jessup's big three-wheeler. Cissy Fry was waiting for me by the gate to the courts. She wore shorts this morning and a white knit shirt, damp already around the collar and under the arms from her warmups.

Cissy opened the gate. "That's Edna Zarrow." She nodded toward the woman hitting the ball against Sharon—a tall, gaunt woman, all bones and skin, with an oversized jaw and curly black hair. "Not much style there," Cissy admitted. "But she's a fine player. She fits right into our game."

"Yes," I said abstractedly. "She told me." I'd never seen Edna Zarrow before—but I had talked on the phone to her and her husband half a dozen times last August, when the Zarrows rented my house.

None of the three, obviously, knew about Scotty.

"Before we start," I said. "I have something you ought to know. It's not good—it's terrible news."

Sharon and Edna stopped their volleying and came over to the bench where I was fumbling with the laces on my sneakers.

"What's happened, Lily?" Sharon asked. "I knew there was something; I saw the police on the beach."

"It's Scotty," I said. "He's dead. Someone put a

bullet in his chest and left him in the water to drown. Somebody murdered Scotty."

"Murdered!" Sharon breathed. She snatched off her dark glasses and blinked in the sun like some nocturnal animal caught by a flashlight beam.

Cissy Fry straightened her back, centered her body, and asked, very carefully, "Why would anyone want to kill Scotty?"

"Nobody knows."

The three of them stared at me.

"Oh, I hate this place!" Sharon blurted out. "It's so dangerous! Terrible thunderstorms coming up without any warning and lightning right on top of you with no place to hide!" She tore off her tennis hat and began to twist it.

"Put your hat on, Sharon," I ordered.

"And the ocean!" she said wildly. "Crashing all night long when you can't see how big the waves are, and you can't tell when they're going to pour over the dune and drown us all! I want to go someplace solid and safe," she wailed. "Someplace where there aren't any murderers running around."

"Cover up," I said sharply.

She sniffed, like a child, and obeyed me.

"When did it happen?" Cissy's voice was matter-of-fact, almost careless. She sat motionless on the bench, her hands resting in her lap, her face expressionless. Only her eyes were guarded.

"Last night, sometime after nine-thirty."

"How come you know so much?" She sounded anxious now.

"Will Mortimer and I found the body. Well, Will pulled it—him—out of the water, but I was there. And now the Suffolk County head of homicide—a man I know, a friend of my brother's—is in charge. Cissy, he's coming to talk to you. I told him you had the homeowners' list."

Edna Zarrow's large jaw hung open as if it had become unhinged. "The police are here? Are they going to talk to *everybody*?"

"I'm sure they'll want to see your daughter. Didn't she have a date with Scotty last night?"

"Yes, but Scotty stood her up. My husband had to walk her over to the party in Fair Harbor. He wasn't gone any time at all," she added quickly. "He came right back."

Sharon stood up. "I have to go. I want to tell the kids about Scotty before my in-laws come on the nine-thirty boat. Mark will have nightmares! I will too," she added, biting her lip, glancing at the sign-up schedule on the fence. "I want to play today. I *need* to play!" she wailed. "Oh, I know you think I'm terrible to want a game with Scotty dead and all that. But tennis is the only thing that keeps me going when I'm really upset."

Edna brightened. "I'll play." She went behind the bench and studied the schedule. "Four o'clock this afternoon?"

"Put me down," Cissy said.

I shook my head. "Sorry."

"We need a fourth." Sharon turned to Cissy. "How about Paula? Is she coming back today?"

"She didn't say," Cissy said. "Oh, sign her up anyway. If she doesn't get back by the middle of the afternoon, I'll ask one of the men to fill in." She picked up her towel and racquet. "Coming, Lily?" Her eyes were guarded again.

"No. I have to meet Lieutenant Bell. He said to tell you we'd be over for the lists about nine-thirty."

Will stood just outside the gate, talking in a low voice to the Rosen brothers.

"Oh, no!" Herb gasped.

Arnold, gray-faced, hands shaking, reached for his cigarettes.

A moment later, Taki appeared, and Will repeated his story.

"It's awful." Taki's voice broke.

I came over to the gate. "Think how awful it's going to be for Jimmy Milgrim," I said. "He's out fishing with the d'Angelos and doesn't know about Scotty—and his mother's off the island. Oh, Taki, will you tell him? And try and help?"

"Of course I will. I'm going home now. I'll be sitting out on my back deck where I can see him when he comes up the walk from the boat slips." He sighed. "It's awful," he said again, and his eyes filled with tears.

So did mine. I wiped them with a tennis sock.

I hoped I'd have a chance to talk to Will, but Edna hung around, and he went into his house.

She sidled up to me. "Lily," she whispered, "will the police want to see everybody?"

"Go home, Edna," I said gently. "Have a cup of coffee and take it easy. If the police want to see you, they'll let you know."

I stowed my sneakers and racquet in the basket of my bike and walked across Center to the blue house on the corner. The door opened, and Harry Bell stepped out on the deck. He motioned for me to join him.

11

HARRY WAVED ME into the house. Carl, his back to us, leaned against the arm of the Ballous' comfortable old couch, explaining something to Fred Mulloy. The young detective stood between a faded brown-canvas director's chair and a rocker with a cane seat. Behind Fred, in the corner by the sliding glass doors, was a child's wooden play pen, littered with toys. Neither man paid the slightest attention to the German shepherd, barking wildly in one of the rear bedrooms.

Harry said, "Do something about that dog!"

Carl yelled through the wall, "Shut up, stupid!" The dog growled and was still. Carl turned, blinking at the square of sunlight in the doorway. As I passed him— close enough to smell the sour perspiration on his crumpled tee shirt and the stale beer on his breath—his face, still blurred with sleep, registered mild surprise and then not-so-mild anger.

"What the hell's she doing here?"

Harry said, "I see you know Mrs. Lambert," and pulled out a chair for me by the round dining table.

"She's got no business in my house."

"Cool it," Harry snapped. "Mrs. Lambert stays." He opened his notebook on the kitchen table.

Fred Mulloy said, "Mr. Hayes, here, says he left Fire Island yesterday afternoon with his wife and child. The little girl was sick, and they took her to the doctor in North Bellmore."

"What time did you leave?" Harry asked.

Carl shrugged. "About three, I guess."

"On the three-forty-five ferry—the *Isle of Fire*," I offered. "I happened to see them. I was walking the dog."

Harry frowned and tapped the pencil on the rungs of his notebook, and I wished I'd kept my mouth shut.

"Mind if I smoke?" Carl reached for cigarettes and matches among the dirty glasses and empty beer cans on the wooden coffee table. Ignoring me, he offered his pack to the men, who shook their heads.

"So you took your kid to the doctor," Harry reminded him.

"In North Bellmore." Carl lit up and inhaled. "A couple of blocks from my in-laws. The guy kept us waiting a long time." He blew smoke up to the ceiling. "Then I left my wife and kid at the in-laws', drove back to the terminal, had a couple of beers and a bite to eat at Porky's, and caught the ferry back here. The eight-thirty ferry." He grinned. Then he frowned. "It was the damndest ferry ride I ever had. Took over an hour. The storm broke just as we pulled into Kismet. Lightning flashing, bright as daylight. Thunder so loud you couldn't hear yourself think. The ferry stayed at the Kismet dock until the storm blew over. We didn't get to Sharon's Landing until a quarter to ten, I guess."

"And then you went home?" Fred asked.

Carl nodded.

"I had to feed the dog and let him out for a minute. I was going to grab a beer and go to bed, but since the wife wasn't around, I decided to go to Ocean Beach and look for a little excitement. So I walked back to the dock hoping I'd catch the ferry that goes up and down the island. It should have come already, according to the schedule, but I figured it was running late because of the storm, and I was right. I got to the dock just in time. By

ten-thirty I was sitting on a bar stool in Sis Norton's."
He sucked on his cigarette.

"Okay. I told you everything." He hooked his thumbs
in his belt loops and let his paunch ride over the top of his
jeans. "Now tell me why you're bothering me."

"You had a fight with Scotty Banks."

"Yeah." He gave a short laugh. "About a baby-sitter.
Yesterday morning."

"And have you seen him since?"

"I sure have." Carl grinned. "Last night. In a bar in
Ocean Beach. He was drunk—real drunk—slobbering
over a broad twice his age and feeling her up." His eyes
mocked me.

"Which bar?"

Carl shrugged.

"Sis Norton's? McGuire's? The Sandpiper?"

Carl couldn't remember. And he couldn't remember
what time it had been, either. "Kind of late, I think. Just
before closing."

Harry said, "You're lying. Scotty was dead by then.
Somebody killed him right after the storm."

"Is that so?" Carl scratched his head. "Is that so?"
He thought a minute. "Then maybe I didn't see him last
night. Maybe it was Friday night."

Or maybe, I suspected, it was never. But why was he
lying? I didn't have a glimmer of an idea.

Carl blinked and tried to concentrate. "Are you setting
me up? You think *I* killed him?"

"Maybe yes, maybe no." Harry closed his notebook.
"Just don't leave the island until we say you can."

Carl pulled himself off the Ballous' old couch and went
into the kitchen for a can of beer. We left him drinking his
breakfast. As we started down the ramp, I glanced
across the walk at the Mortimers' pink house. Judging by
the evidence—drawn shades at the side windows, curtains still covering the glass-walled living room facing the
triangle of sand on the corner—Caroline Mortimer was

sleeping late this morning. Maybe, I thought nervously, because she didn't sleep much last night.

Harry stopped when we reached the walk and put his hand on my arm. "Lily, don't tangle with Carl Hayes. A man like that could make trouble for you."

"I'll keep my distance," I promised.

He took his hand back as Will came around the corner from Center.

Will nodded to us.

Harry scowled at his watch. "Nine-fifty," he muttered. "I'll meet you at the Frys' as soon as Fred and I take care of some business." He turned and strode up Beach Plum with the young detective.

Will rolled his bicycle out of the new rack by his ramp, wheeled it down to Center, and disappeared around the corner. After a minute, when the two detectives were out of sight, I followed him. He was standing at the edge of the walk on a line with the poison ivy patch behind Carl's house—facing me as I approached, keeping his eye on the front deck of his own house. Nobody stirred at Fredericka Borg's, whose backyard abutted Carl's. Across the walk, the thick screen of Japanese pines surrounding the courts kept the players from seeing us. Center itself was deserted.

"What were you doing there with the police?" he asked anxiously.

"I'm supposed to be helping them. Showing them around."

"Good." He nodded. "You'll know what's going on."

"Have you talked to Caroline?"

"Not yet. She was sleeping when I came in at seven, and I haven't been home since." He frowned and looked anxious again. "Why hasn't Bell come around to see her?"

"I don't know. Maybe he's trying to get the feel of the place first. Or maybe he's waiting for some information. From the medical examiner or somebody."

"Of course!" He brightened a little, but I didn't.

"Do you think Caroline suspects anything?" I asked. "You were gone all night! If she woke and you weren't there and she happened to remember seeing us together—"

"Oh, Lily!" he said softly. "Don't worry about *that!*" He reached out to touch my face and then stopped himself. "I'm called out at night lots of times. She expects it."

"But doesn't she know when you leave? Doesn't the phone wake her when it rings?"

"Most of the time." His voice went flat. "But not when she's sleeping off a drunk." He pursed his lips and stared at the front deck of his house. "Come on. We better move." We started walking toward Blueberry, on either side of his bike. "I'm going to the store for the *Times*, but I'll be right back. Tell your friend Bell. I don't want him to talk to Caroline unless I'm there. And don't worry about that other thing, Lily. You hear?" he drawled and gave me the kind of smile that made me catch my breath. Then he mounted his bike and rode off.

If I run to catch a ferry, I can make it from Center to the dock in two minutes flat. But I wasn't in a hurry this time. I strolled down Blueberry, listening to the twang of tennis balls and the murmur of voices drifting through the Japanese pines on my right. On my left, three houses lined the walk. I waved to Mary d'Angelo, who was watering the begonias by her ramp, and nodded to Herb Rosen, her next-door neighbor, who passed me on his bike. Herb's brother, Arnold, owned the third house; Arnold's living room looked out on the dock and a portion of Crescent Walk, a brief half-circle of concrete behind the tiny bay beach.

A ferry was due. Seven or eight people waited with empty wagons, their backs to me, gazing out across the calm, blue bay. Sunlight lacquered the glassy surface of the water. Dozens of power boats dotted the fishing area beyond Kismet—some of them ours, I figured, for all the slips below the bulkhead were empty. So was the bay beach to the left of the dock—a sliver of sand at the edge of the swimming area. Scotty's bailiwick.

I stopped at the foot of Blueberry and stared at the empty beach. Sorrow sneaked up on me, but I ignored it; I had some heavy thinking to do. I stuck my hands in the pocket of my tennis shorts and considered, for a start, what I knew about Scotty's killer.

It wasn't much. Only that he or she lived in Sharon's Landing; no outsider would have been wearing a work shirt with one of our tennis tags hooked onto the pocket flap. That gave me forty suspects, more or less. Quite a crowd, I acknowledged; but I could probably eliminate the Van Burens and Elmo Kesselbaum, who never played tennis, and Matilda Huff, who was too old for the game. The police, checking who was where on Saturday night, might trim the number further. And some people, of course, were more suspect than others. I carried around a list of them in my head:

Leo Milgrim. I never met Leo; I didn't know what kind of man he was, and I wouldn't even try to guess whether he killed Scotty. But I bet he wanted to. How could he bear to have Scotty living in his house, growing closer and closer to his stepson and probably sleeping with his wife?

Caroline Mortimer. In spite of what I had told Harry Bell—and Will—Caroline worried me with her drinking and her threats and her unreasonable anger. For a while, I reminded myself grimly, even her husband thought she pulled the trigger.

June Milgrim. June hadn't been upset by her argument with Scotty on the tennis court—but Scotty didn't like it one bit. If he threatened to leave her board and bed—and her child—she might have shot him, although it seemed far-fetched. But then, I didn't really know just how intense their relationship was.

I added Al Fry to my list because I had seen him doing something suspicious and out of character—peering through his binoculars into June Milgrim's bedroom. Why, I wondered. Was June his secret passion? Could he have killed Scotty because he was jealous of him?

Carl Hayes, that bad-tempered, dangerous man could have blown up at Scotty. If he had a gun. I could picture him pulling the trigger in cold blood. But I put him last among the suspects because of the tennis tag. I doubted whether he or his wife had ever set foot on the courts. Even if he owned a work shirt, he wouldn't have attached a tennis tag to it. I thought about that for a moment and changed my mind about Carl; he belonged near the top of my list. He wouldn't own a work shirt with a tag attached, but he might have borrowed one. From his landlord. Dan Ballou might have left his own shirt behind in a closet, perhaps, or hanging on a nail in the storage shed on the side deck.

It was possible—and that pleased me. We had a long way to go before we solved Scotty's murder. But I hoped, with all my heart, that when we found the killer, he'd turn out to be Carl Hayes.

I took my hands out of my pockets and glanced at my watch. It was almost ten—time for the first ferry to make its appearance. The bay beach had a couple of visitors now: three-year-old Patti Girard, in a white piqué bonnet and the bottom half of a red bikini, let go of her mother's hand, squatted at the edge of the water, and began to fill her red plastic pail with wet sand. Beyond Patti and her mother, out beyond the empty swimming area and the flats, where a pair of clammers bent to their work, the *Firefly* cut through the bright, still water, maneuvered the last curve in the channel, and nestled against the dock. Fifteen or twenty passengers debarked—all visitors, I noted automatically, except for Pete Raymond, a political writer (and my favorite partner for mixed doubles) and Elmo Kesselbaum, who was Sharon's Landing's only bachelor over twenty-five.

The dock emptied quickly. Sharon Jessup, her in-laws in tow, nodded a greeting. Brian and Jo-Ellen MacKay, pulling a wagon full of bundles, passed me with their guests—an Asian couple and their two young children.

"All aboard," the deckhand called. "All aboard for Bay Shore."

Someone behind me brushed against my arm. I turned, and a pale, stooped man, his jaw shadowed by dark stubble, muttered, "I'm terribly sorry," and rushed onto the dock and into the ferry. He was the only passenger returning to the mainland this holiday weekend morning. I wondered who he was and why he had to leave the beach in such a hurry that he didn't have time to shave. Something about him seemed familiar. I was trying to puzzle it out when Pete Raymond walked off the dock in front of me.

Pete took an unlighted cigar out of his mouth, said "Hi ya, Lily!" in his gravelly voice, and gave me a big hug.

I hugged him back. "Where you been, Pete?"

"East Hampton. To a wedding. My agent tied the knot for the fourth time, poor guy. We left here last night after the thunderstorm. Wasn't it something?"

I nodded.

"Elmo and I waited half an hour for the goddamn ferry!" he went on. "We boarded looking like a couple of drowned rats!" He felt for his matches in the pockets of his jeans. "El was best man. This time and last time, too." He looked around. "El? Where are you?"

Elmo Kesselbaum, a small, shy man with a bushy brown beard and no hair at all on his head, appeared behind two mountainous backpackers who stopped and asked him—of all people—how to get down to the beach. Elmo never swam in the ocean, or sunned, or fished, or walked by the water (or partied or played tennis, either); every day, June through September, he sat at his word processor and worked, turning out one torrid romance each summer he lived here—each title a woman's name: *Helena, Cassandra, Rita, Janet, Lydia.*

Elmo shook my hand and said soberly, "Welcome back, Lily."

I thanked him and asked Pete, "Where's Calley?" Pete's wife was an environmental biologist.

"Colorado Springs. She had to make a speech." Pete puffed up like a blowfish. "Almost a thousand people heard her." He lit his cigar. "What's new here? Anything happen while we were gone?"

"See you later," I mumbled. I couldn't bear to tell them about Scotty. And Harry Bell, coming from Holly Walk to the west of us, had turned onto Crescent. I caught up with him just as he started to climb the ramp to the Frys' house.

12

THE DANCER ON the far side of the Frys' living room rested her left hand on the back of a kitchen chair and bent her right knee in preparation for a turn. Perspiration matted her sepia hair and glistened on her pale nude body.

Harry Bell strode across the room, put on his glasses, and studied the large blue bruise above her right elbow, the varicose veins forming a spidery skull-and-cross-bones on the inside of her left thigh, and the x-ray view of both knees, bared by Al Fry (who had painted the dancer ten years ago) to show muscle, tendon, bone, and blood.

Cissy Fry, in a yellow shirt and jeans—matchstick-thin, showing off the shape of her beautiful legs—stood by the round dining table watching him, her hands clasped in front of her. She was nervous; the longer he stared, the tighter she squeezed her hands—and that bothered me. I'm very fond of Cissy.

Harry turned and peered at her over the top of his glasses. "May we sit down?"

"Of course! I'm sorry!" She unclasped her hands to pull out a chair for herself and to motion for us to join her at the table.

Harry sat between us. He nodded at the dancer. "You were the model, Mrs. Fry?"

"How could you tell?" I asked. "Al distorted the body, and he hid the face. What made you think it was Cissy?"

"The *Newsweek* cover story on Mr. Fry."

"That article came out two years ago. How could you remember?"

"I studied it carefully. I like to know all I can about people who live in my territory."

"It was a good article," Cissy admitted. "Even Al said so." She glanced at the charcoal drawing hanging on the wall by the kitchen—Al's sketch of his own round head, round body, round metal-framed glasses, round penetrating eyes. Those eyes looking at us mirrored a shrewd, cocky, exuberant man—not exactly your ordinary, run-of-the-mill voyeur, I thought. Weren't Peeping Toms supposed to be shy creeps who were afraid to speak to women?

Harry said, "Now that's the kind of picture I understand." He nodded toward a watercolor of Al's sailboat at anchor ten feet offshore. Behind it, a long, low island floated on the palcid water. It was an exact replica of what I saw through the Frys' sliding glass door this morning.

"Al's boat is out there. Didn't he go sailing?"

She shook her head. "He's sick. A stomach virus or something."

"Have you called a doctor?" I asked.

"He won't let me." She bit her lip. "He's terrified of doctors. Hasn't been to one in years."

Harry said, "We won't keep you long, Mrs. Fry."

She opened a folder on the table and gave him two sheets of paper stapled together. "This is our homeowners' list. The local phone number's under each name. The next column has the home address and business addresses. The third column has all the city phone numbers. You can keep it—I have plenty of copies—and the one of the renters, too." She took out a second list. "Herb Rosen and his family are renting for the whole season. Right next door to his brother Arnold. This is their third summer out here. The Zarrows have the Poole

94

house for July, and the Hayes couple took the Ballou house from June thirtieth to July fifteenth. The other people on the list will be renting for August only."

"Thank you. This is exactly what we need." Harry folded the lists and put them in the back of his notebook. Then he smiled at Cissy and said, "Tell me what you know about Scotty Banks."

"It's not much, I'm afraid. I hired him to teach our swimming classes three years ago. Paula Wohlens recommended him. He was one of her students at New York University. His references—from the Albany YMCA—were outstanding. We rehired him automatically the next two seasons."

"Any complaints?"

She shook her head. "He was a great teacher."

"He taught tennis too?"

"Yes. A couple of classes mid-day. We paid him to teach the group lessons, to maintain the bayfront swimming area, and to take care of the courts. He pocketed the fees for private lessons both places. Everything else he did without pay."

"Everything else?"

"When anybody needed a baby-sitter or a kid to scrape the deck or help out at a party, Scotty arranged it. He had a knack for picking the right kids for the right jobs."

"Do you know anything about his family?"

She shook her head, "Ask Paula Wohlens or her husband, John. John comes from Albany too, and I think he knows the family. Call them in the city. They left here last night on the eight twenty-five ferry from Fair Harbor."

"From Fair Harbor?"

She nodded. "The Saturday night boat in and out of Sharon's Landing is the *Isle of Fire*. Paula's afraid to ride on it at night or in rough weather—she was stuck on it, once, for an hour, when it's engine failed in the middle of the open bay."

He peered at her over his glasses. "How do you know which ferry they caught?"

"My husband and the MacKays saw them board. What difference does it make?"

"We have to know everyone's comings and goings last night. Even yours."

"We went to a party in Saltaire," she said promptly. "Pam and Wally Wallace invited us for dinner. They're the gallery owners on Fifty-seventh Street where Al shows." She smiled at Harry and folded her hands in her lap. "Oh." Her smile faded. "You want to know when we left home and how long we stayed and all that."

He nodded.

"Minute by minute?"

He nodded again.

She leaned back in her chair and crossed her legs. "Brian and Jo-Ellen MacKay came by for us about twenty to eight. We were walking; Saltaire doesn't allow bikes after dark. On the way, we stopped in Fair Harbor. I went to the grocery store to order some meat, while Al and the MacKays went around the corner to the liquor store to buy wine for the Wallaces. Then we walked to Saltaire by way of Center. The Wallaces have an old brown house right on the bay, on the other side of the Saltaire dock. We arrived at quarter to nine."

"When did you leave the party?"

She hesitated for the first time. "The MacKays and I stayed until almost midnight. We came back on the lateral ferry. But Al left almost as soon as we arrived. On the walk over, he complained about his stomach feeling strange, and the minute we walked in the door, he asked Wally for a brandy." She frowned. "Al never drinks except on airplanes when there's turbulence and he gets nervous. Anyway, he gulped down the drink. Then he told Wally and me he felt achy and wanted to leave. Wally noticed one of the boats from Island Taxi approaching the dock—you know, the lateral taxis that tear up and down the bay. They had room for Al. They zipped him home in five minutes, just before the storm broke. He called me at 9:30, when the lights went back on, to say he was feeling better, and I should stay." She frowned. "But he's still sick!"

Harry said, "We'd like to talk to your husband. Would you tell him, please?"

"No." Cissy stiffened her back. "I don't want to disturb him unless you tell me I have to. He was up all night, and he didn't fall asleep until just before you came."

"Let him sleep. But call me at Mrs. Lambert's right away when he wakes up."

Cissy rose and walked with me to the door.

"May I use your phone, Mrs. Fry?" Harry asked.

She nodded.

He went into the kitchen and dialed a number. When he began to talk, he turned his back to us.

"Cissy," I moved close to her. "How long has Al known June Milgrim?" I spoke calmly, softly—but I caught her off guard.

"What?" She stared at me. "How did you—" She ran her tongue over her lips.

"Tell me," I insisted. "Now." I motioned toward the kitchen. "While he's busy."

She swallowed and said, "June posed for Al about five years ago. Just for a few weeks." Her voice was low and dull; her eyes never left Harry's back. "He did a few drawings of her and two oils—terrible, mawkish things, not like him at all. Wally sold them to some Saudi Arabian." She licked her lips again. "But Al never saw her after that until she turned up in Sharon's Landing." She squeezed her hands together. "Oh, Lily," she whispered, "it can't have anything to do with the murder! Please don't tell the police!"

"I won't," I promised. "Not unless I have to."

Harry hung up and said, "The red tennis tags. Do you still have yours, Mrs. Fry?"

She shook her head. "I threw them out two years ago when we painted. But why—"

"That's all, then," Harry said. "Thank you for your help."

As we left the Frys' house, a seaplane banked above us, landed on the open water, and skiied toward our dock. We turned off Crescent onto Blueberry and stopped by Arnold Rosen's ramp, watching the plane pull up and the pilot help a passenger alight. A female passenger, in baggy jeans, sweatshirt, huge sunglasses, and a head scarf hugging her cheeks.

"It's June Milgrim. In her traveling clothes," I explained.

June left the dock and walked over to us. "Hi, Lily. What a nice day they gave us!" She untied her scarf, pushed her sunglasses up through her copper hair, and smiled shyly at me and at Harry.

I did the honors—all of them. "June Milgrim, this is Lieutenant Bell from the police. From the homicide department. He's here because we've had a tragedy. Scotty's dead. Drowned."

"Scotty Banks?" She shook her head. "No! No, Lily, you must be mistaken. I played tennis with him yesterday—you saw us!" she insisted, her voice rising. "And Scotty had all kinds of plans with Jimmy for today—even if it rained." She swallowed suddenly. "Scotty was teaching him chess." Her eyes widened with fright. "Is my son—"

"He doesn't know yet; he's out fishing on the d'Angelos' boat," I said. "I asked Taki to tell him and talk about it with him. I hope you don't mind. Taki Andreapolis is one of the best child psychiatrists in the city."

"Thank you, Lily." She reached for my hand. "Jimmy and I thank you."

We had passed Arnold Rosen's side yard and the house his brother Herb was renting and the ramp to the d'Angelos' deck—as far as the Russian olive bushes, silver-green in the clear morning air—when June stopped abruptly, her face gray with fear.

"Jimmy won't be able to bear it! Everyone's dead— his father and my fiancé. And now Scotty. Everybody he ever loved!"

"You're here, Mrs. Milgrim," Harry said soberly. "And your husband."

She shook her head. "Not Leo. He and Jimmy don't get along. Leo's too impatient. Oh, Lily," she pleaded, "what am I going to do?"

"Why don't you ask Taki? Right now? He's sitting on his back deck, waiting for Jimmy to come home."

She sighed. "I guess I better."

Harry took her arm. "We'll go with you."

As we climbed the rise on the other side of Center, Harry asked, "Mrs. Milgrim, can you get in touch with your husband?"

She shook her head. "He's at the Hilton in the city seeing a client from out of town. I don't know the client's name. But Leo's coming back to Fire Island this afternoon." She sighed wearily and stopped to wipe her eyes. Her color was better, but her eyes looked sad and haunted. "How could he drown? A good swimmer like Scotty?"

Harry, watching her closely, said, "Somebody shot him first and left him at the edge of the water. The tide was coming in."

"Shot him?" she repeated. "With a gun? Who'd do something like that? Her eyes glazed, and I thought, she's denying his death again. She's trying to make it go away.

She shuddered and said harshly, "I hate guns! Leo wanted to bring his revolver out to Fire Island, but I told him not to." Then she dropped a bombshell right in my lap. "Lily, did you tell the lieutenant about Caroline Mortimer's gun?"

I stared at her. "What are you talking about?"

"The gun she was waving around yesterday afternoon. I thought you saw it too," she said apologetically.

Harry said, "What time yesterday?"

"About a quarter to five. When Lily and I left the courts. Caroline was sitting at the redwood table in the corner of her deck. She had the gun in her hand and suddenly she pointed it at me. I was terrified—but then she caught my eye and laughed and put it down. It was a big black gun."

"Why do you think she pointed it at you?"

"I don't have the slightest idea. You'd better ask her yourself."

We left June with Taki, and Harry and I walked to the Mortimers'. Will met us at the foot of his ramp.

"Lieutenant Bell," he said, "I woke my wife half an hour ago. I told her about Scotty, and about you, and I said that I wanted her to get a lawyer."

Harry nodded. "I think that's wise, Doctor."

"But Caroline wouldn't even consider it! She insists . . ."

We didn't get to hear what she insisted, for Caroline herself interrupted him, calling "Good mornin', good mornin' " from the deck of her house.

13

SHE WAS WEARING a pair of faded jeans, the crimson shirt I'd seen her in the day before, a dash of crimson lipstick, and a haughty smile. I had to admire her. Caroline Mortimer is the only woman I know who can manage to look regal when she's barefoot and hung over.

"Lily, is that your friend from the police?"

I nodded. "Lieutenant Bell."

"Come up here, Lieutenant," she commanded. "I want to talk to you."

Harry climbed up the ramp with Will. I followed, after a moment, dragging my feet because I knew (and dreaded) what Caroline was going to tell Harry: Everything. Her feelings, her fantasies, all the details of her life—without the slightest bit of editing.

"Come inside," Caroline groaned "so I can open my eyes."

We walked into the house. I dragged my feet again, wishing we could have stayed on the deck. Though I'd been in the Mortimers' living room dozens of times before, it bothered me this time. I felt like an invader looking over the property I was about to despoil.

"Sit there, Lieutenant." Caroline motioned toward the pseudo-leather Italian couch that backs up against the far wall, and I remembered when she bought the couch. I noticed that the new bookcases in the corner were half-filled already (the Mortimers are both voracious readers) and that Will's tennis racquet and balls lay on the dining table where he had dropped them when he came in from the courts. Since I hoped to steal her husband, these scenes from Caroline's marriage made me feel guilty as hell. And envious too. I wanted Will to drop his tennis things on *my* dining table.

"Coffee anyone?" Caroline asked. When we shook our heads, she said, "I'll be right with you." Moving into the kitchen, she measured instant coffee into a mug and poured in water from the tea kettle whistling on the stove.

I picked a canvas chair and sat down on it. Will elected to stand by the living room windows.

Caroline carried her coffee to the low wood table in front of the sofa, brought over a chair from the dining table, and seated herself so close to Harry that her knees almost touched his.

"Lieutenant Bell," she confided, "Will doesn't want me to say a word to you until I talk to a lawyer."

"That's not a bad idea, Mrs. Mortimer."

"Please, Caroline," Will pleaded. "Let me call Jo-Ellen MacKay. She'd be glad—"

"I told you. I don't want a lawyer." Caroline tossed her head, flipping clouds of honey-blonde hair. "I hated Scotty Banks! I'm glad he's dead, and I don't care who knows it."

She expected to shock Harry and possibly me. But only her husband reacted. He began pacing back and forth in front of the door.

She tried again. "I'm only sorry your killer didn't shoot June Milgrim too!"

Harry crossed one leg over the other and leaned back and asked calmly, "Know anything about guns, Mrs. Mortimer?"

"I sure do." She drew herself up proudly. "I'm a southern woman, Lieutenant Bell. My daddy taught me to shoot when I was twelve. With his own Colt .45 from World War I. His daddy carried it in France."

"The same gun you pointed at Mrs. Milgrim?"

"Yes," she said heavily, "the same gun."

"Why did you bring it to Fire Island?"

"I didn't know I was bringing it. I'd been back home to Arkansas, finishing up some business. My daddy died two months ago." She paused and waited for us to fill in our own picture of her dressed in black, grieving at the grave.

"I flew back to New York on Friday," she continued, "and Will picked me up at the airport. Since we drove straight out to the ferry terminal, I had to bring everything to Fire Island—my suitcase and a big old suitcase of Daddy's that had a briefcase full of papers inside, and his medical bag, and his old metal file box. Friday night, after dinner, when Will was out, I opened the file box. The gun was sitting on top of all the files."

"And on Saturday, you removed the gun, brought it out on your deck, and pointed it at Mrs. Milgrim. Why?"

"It couldn't hurt anybody," she said, ignoring his question. "It was empty."

"Did you point the gun at anyone else?"

She shook her head.

"Did you shoot Scotty Banks?"

"No." She grinned defiantly. "I only wish I'd had the pleasure." She drained her mug and set it on the table.

"When did this fortuitous event take place?"

"We're not sure, yet." Harry opened his notebook. "Sometime after nine-thirty last night. Where were you when the storm ended?"

"At E. J. Warner's house on Oak Walk in Fair Harbor, where our women's group met. The meeting broke up early. As soon as the lights went back on, everybody left, except two of us who stayed to help E. J. clean up. It took us about fifteen or twenty minutes. Then I walked back to Sharon's Landing on the beach."

"Alone?" Harry asked.

"All alone."

"How long did it take you?"

She shrugged. *"You* figure how long it took in a heavy fog, when I had to walk through loose sand up by the dune so as not to miss my own beach stairs and end up in Point O'Woods—or some place. Then I made myself a bottle of martinis and sat myself down on the beach steps to polish them off—and turned sick. Lily took me home; she was outside, doing something under the corner of her house, and she caught me with the beam of her flashlight." She frowned and looked puzzled. "I don't know what happened after that."

Harry opened his notebook. "Do you have Ms. Warner's phone number?"

"It's 280-7402." Caroline smiled graciously, the queen giving an audience. "Anything else you want to know?"

"Why did you bring the gun out on your deck?"

"To shoot at seagulls," she snapped. But her eyes wavered; her defiance was only half-hearted.

"Tell me," Harry said.

"Please, Caroline," Will pleaded. "Let me call Jo-Ellen."

She ignored him, battling with herself. Her body slumped suddenly. "What difference does it make if I tell you?" She focused on the crimson imprint of her lips on the white coffee mug. "I got the idea when I came off the beach yesterday, about three, and stopped by the courts to sign up for Sunday morning. I glanced at the Saturday schedule first—Sunday was underneath—and noticed that at four o'clock, June was playing doubles, and Scotty had a private lesson. I decided to scare them a little when they came off the courts. Maybe even scare them a lot. I wasn't going to shoot them or anything." She flushed and looked away. "The gun wasn't loaded— Daddy kept the bullets in a pouch in the file box. I was just going to point the gun at them. I hoped they'd be frightened out of their wits!"

"Caroline!" Will exploded.

She ignored him. "I went home and put on this red shirt to attract their attention, and found Will and sent him clamming in the bay to get him out of the house. At about four-thirty, I made myself a martini and carried it out with the gun and *The New York Times* to the table in the corner of my deck. Just as I sat down, the phone rang. I covered the gun with the *Times,* went in the house and took a complicated message from Will's service. On my way back, I stopped off in the bathroom. I wasn't inside more than fifteen minutes—my drink was still cold, though the ice had melted. But when I came out, there was Scotty, going down Center. I thought I'd missed my chance, but he could have been scared by my gun. The wind had blown the *Times* off the table and left the gun uncovered.

"As things happened, it didn't really matter whether or not he'd seen it, because June was terrified when I pointed the gun at her, and I knew she'd tell him about it."

Caroline looked out the window, blinking at the sunlight. "I guess you think I'm crazy, Lieutenant. But you have to understand what a wonderful girl Millie was—a straight-A student in high school with fabulous scores on her S.A.T.'s. She was ready to start at Penn—all packed and everything—when Scotty Banks dumped her like a bag of garbage and ruined her life!"

"Are you done, Caroline?" Will said angrily. "Are you finished telling Lieutenant Bell your fantasies?"

Caroline said, "Now, Will . . ."

"Let me tell you about my daughter." Will stopped pacing and seated himself on the edge of the sofa, facing Harry. "She's a wonderful girl, and I love her very much. But she was not a straight-A student. As her mother well knows, there were B's sprinkled among her A's, and two or three C's. One in chemistry, if I remember correctly. And her S.A.T.'s weren't what you'd call fabulous, as her mother claims." He glared at Caroline. "Though they were good enough to get her into three or four fine small colleges—Haverford was her first choice—and the University of Pennsylvania, where her mother insisted she apply and then insisted she attend."

"Penn has more prestige than the others," Caroline argued, "and that would have helped when she applied to medical school."

He sighed and shook his head. "How many times did Millie tell you that she was not going to be a doctor? Fifty times? A hundred times?"

Caroline scowled into her mug. "Once she was at Penn, she might have changed her mind."

"Lieutenant Bell, Millie is a pretty good student, a talented watercolorist, a lovely ballet dancer—but no doctor, no matter how hard her mother tries to make her into one." Will stood up and began pacing again. "Oh, I'm as much to blame as Caroline. I should have insisted that Millie make her own choices. But I was working twice as hard as usual at just the wrong time, and I left everything to my wife."

Harry said, "Are you telling me that it was all a family problem? That Scotty Banks had nothing to do with your daughter leaving town?"

"I don't know." Will scratched the sunburn on the back of his neck. "Maybe he was the last straw."

Harry cleared his throat. "May I see the gun now, Mrs. Mortimer?"

Caroline stood up and walked down the hall into the bedroom.

Harry said, "I'd like to make a call, Dr. Mortimer."

"Go ahead." Will nodded toward the kitchen phone.

Harry dialed, and I heard him say, "What do you have, Brady?" He listened a minute, hung up, and stood at the counter, pulling on a sideburn. Then he raised his eyebrows and looked at me. Caroline was taking too long. I started to go after her when she appeared in the hallway.

"It's gone. It's not in the file box where I left it." She stared at us, her mouth ugly with fear. "Somebody's stolen my gun."

"Are you sure it's gone?" Harry asked sharply. "Maybe it fell out or you put it someplace else."

"No. I put it back in the file box." She spoke between clenched teeth. "I know I did. Somebody stole it. They took the leather pouch and the bullets, too."

"Did you tell anybody you had a gun? Any of your friends?"

"Nobody!" she said instantly. "Not even Will! He was out Friday night when I opened the file case and found it. I wanted—" She caught herself and swallowed and rubbed her mouth, smearing her chin with lipstick. "I wanted to keep it a secret," she admitted, digging a hole for herself halfway to China.

"Are there any marks on the gun?" Harry asked. "Any way we can identify it?"

"My granddaddy was in the Rainbow Division; he scratched a rainbow design on the handle."

Harry pulled on a sideburn. "When could anybody have taken the gun?"

"The house was empty from seven-thirty on, when I left for my women's group. Will caught the six-thirty ferry for Bay Shore."

"I'd arranged to meet someone at a restaurant on the pier," Will offered. "A friend."

I sucked in my breath and thought, a friend? What kind of friend?

"The wife of an old patient of mine," Will explained. "She wanted my advice about a personal problem."

It occurred to me for the first time that Will might have had other women in his life—and I was stunned by the idea. I blinked and tried to make it go away. When it wouldn't, I tried thinking. Why not? I asked myself. Why shouldn't Will have had a casual affair or two, I reasoned. He and I only got together twelve hours ago. Neither of us had brought up the subject last night. I promised myself I'd bring it up the next time we were alone. Meanwhile, I thought (squirming a little on the canvas chair), there's no need to panic.

"What restaurant?" Harry asked Will.

"The Surf Club."

"How long did you stay?"

"A little over an hour. My friend drove me around to the ferry terminal afterwards. I caught the eight-thirty boat back to Sharon's Landing." He shook his head. "That was the longest ferry trip I ever had—an hour and ten minutes."

"Because of the storm?"

He nodded. "We stopped at Kismet, and we were still there when the storm hit. Thank God! All hell broke loose over Great South Bay!"

"Was the boat crowded?"

"Are you kidding? At eight-thirty on a Saturday night? Maybe ten people got off at Kismet. There were only two of us for Sharon's Landing." He wrinkled his nose. "My companion was Carl Hayes."

"When the ferry arrived, did you go straight home?"

"Yes. Except that I visited with Herb and Arnold Rosen on the walk for a couple of minutes."

"What time did you get home?"

"Ten o'clock. Maybe a quarter of. I didn't notice."

"When you came into the house, was Mrs. Mortimer home?"

"No, she was out."

"Was there any disarray? Did it look like somebody had broken in?"

Will smiled. "Nobody *broke* in. But somebody might have *walked* in. We never lock up. Nobody out here

108

does. Even when we close the house for the winter, we always leave the key hanging on a nail under the eaves right by the door." He frowned thoughtfully for a moment. "If somebody was inside, he didn't leave any traces. I don't remember anything looking different."

Will stared down at his hands for a moment. "Lieutenant Bell," he asked, "what kind of gun did the killer use? Was it a .45?"

"We don't know, yet. We won't know for another half-hour or so." He snapped his notebook shut. "Call me if the gun turns up. I'm temporarily at Mrs. Lambert's."

He smiled pleasantly and started for the door when the phone rang.

Will answered. He listened a moment, said, "Right away," and hung up.

"Who's that?" Caroline asked.

"Cissy Fry. Al's sick. I promised her I'd get right over."

"Dr. Mortimer," Harry said, "would you mind if I came with you? I'd like to talk to Mr. Fry if you think he's well enough."

Will said, "That's fine with me," and went into the bedroom for his bag.

"No need for you to come, Lily," Harry murmured. "I won't be long; I'll see you back at the house; Fred has some things for us."

He hurried out the door with Will.

Which left me alone with Caroline.

"Well," she sighed, "I'm glad that's over." She sank down on the sofa and massaged her temples. "Wasn't Will awful?"

"I'd say he was great." I stood up to leave. "If you could let yourself really think about what he said, you'd understand how pressured Millie must have felt."

Her eyes filled with tears.

"Come on, Caroline," I said. "Guilt is for the birds.

109

The idea is to understand *why* she left, so that when she come back, you won't make the same mistakes all over again."

"Are you sure you don't want any coffee?"

"I've had all I can drink today."

She walked me to the door. "You know, Lily, he's really quite taken with you."

"What?" I said, barely daring to breathe.

"The lieutenant. He likes you. I can always tell about those things." She nodded sagely. "Next time you're with him," she drawled, "put in a good word for your old friend Caroline."

14

I LEFT CAROLINE in her kitchen spooning more coffee out of the jar of instant, crossed Center, and went over to the bicycle rack by the tennis courts. I'd dumped my sneakers and equipment in the basket of my bike a couple of hours before and left them there—even my new Wilson Graphite—without the slightest concern that they'd be stolen. We may have a murderer in Sharon's Landing, but no thieves. Except for bicycle thieves, I reminded myself. Anyone who leaves a bike outside overnight is taking a chance not only that it will rust in the heavy dew, but that it will disappear. Carousers, returning on foot from Ocean Beach, mount any bike they see and ride it home—depositing it afterwards in the high reeds on some deserted corner, where it rusts a lot more and may not be found for weeks, if at all.

I rode home by way of Beach Plum and Ocean, parked my bike in the shed under my ramp, and cleaned out the basket, hurrying a little. The dog needed a walk; I wanted to take him out before Harry Bell returned.

I was starting up the ramp when Jimmy Milgrim turned the corner from Blueberry and called, "Mrs. Lambert!" He carried a fishing pole on his shoulder and lugged, with difficulty, a heavy fishing pail. "Come here!" he called excitedly, the hardware on his teeth flashing. "Come and look at this!"

He set down the pail in the middle of the walk. I went over and peered in at a large, silvery shape moving around in the water.

"Mr. d'Angelo took us out in his boat this morning, and I caught it! Nobody even helped me!" He hopped excitedly from one foot to the other. "Mr. d'Angelo told me to play it some more, but it *felt* like it was hooked good, so I just pulled it in. All by myself." He puffed out his small chest. "I can't wait for Scotty to see it!"

"Oh, no!" I gasped.

"What's the matter?" The boy looked at me curiously.

I was rescued, one more time, by Taki Andreapolis. Newly showered, in a fresh set of tennis whites, his dark, wavy hair combed and shining, Taki strolled up behind us. "What do you have there, Jimmy?"

The boy lifted his pail, and Taki looked inside.

"A bluefish." Taki whistled. "Close to three pounds, I'd say. Good work." He smiled admiringly. "Know how to clean it?"

Jimmy shook his head.

"I'll show you. Come on." He put his hand on the boy's shoulder, and the two of them walked up the Milgrims' ramp.

I opened the sliding glass door to my house, and the policeman at the far end of the living room rose from his chair behind two black telephones side by side on my card table. He was a small-boned man, sandy-haired, not yet thirty, I figured, who must have thought he looked too young and tried to remedy the problem with a thick, shaving-brush mustache.

"What can I do for you?" he asked.

"Not much. I live here."

"Mrs. Lambert!" He smiled, offering me his hand. The ends of his mustache spread out and up toward the tops of his ears. "I'm Sergeant Brady. Glad to know you. We borrowed your card table for the telephones. And I walked your dog. He was scratching at the door. He's a nice dog, for a poodle."

112

Mops, hearing himself talked about, left his post by the card table and thumped his tail at me.

"You have visitors," the Sergeant went on. One of the phones rang. He picked it up and said, "Just a minute." "Out on the deck," he said to me.

On my side deck I found Edna Zarrow, staring at the ocean, her body all bones and skin, huddled in a redwood lounge chair.

"Hello, Edna," I said. "Want a cup of coffee?"

She put her hands on her stomach. "Oh, I couldn't swallow a thing! I'm too upset." Her large, square jaw began to quiver. "About Scotty, I mean."

"Aren't we all?" I pulled up a chair next to her.

"Is that detective here?"

"Lieutenant Bell? No. He had to go talk to somebody. One of his men is here."

She nodded. "That's good." Some of the strain left her face. "My daughter wanted to come over here to see him, but I said she should talk to you instead. She's in the john." Edna nodded toward the back door. "She made herself at home. I hope you don't mind."

"Of course not! She has a right to. She lived here for a month last summer. Edna, I don't know whether I ever really thanked you for taking such good care of my house. Not every renter would have, you know."

Her bony face colored with pleasure. "But it's such a lovely home!"

"You had a good time here, didn't you?"

"It was the nicest vacation I ever had! In my whole life! I could hardly believe it was me sitting out here and looking at the ocean whenever I wanted to, without a million other people around, the way it is at Jones Beach. Or at Coney Island, where I went when I was a child and we lived in Brooklyn." She smiled wistfully. "I just had to come back this year! Renting out here costs more money than we ought to spend—but we think it's worth every penny! 'Three tennis courts,' I told my friends! And all the people are so nice and so, well, intellectual—reading and playing chess all the time. It's a very good atmosphere for Ramona."

Edna glanced at the back door again. "Ramona wanted to talk to you alone, but I didn't think it was right," she said earnestly. "She's still a child. My husband would have come, but he had to leave on the first ferry this morning. Business."

"What does he do?" I asked. The rental agent had told me last summer, but I'd forgotten.

"Oh, it was family business, why he left. I mean, his sister's ill," she added hurriedly, her square jaw quivering with alarm. She clamped her teeth together, and when the quivering stopped, she said, "Helmut's in advertising. And I'm in *education*!" She pronounced the word with the reverence some people reserve for God. "Administrative aide to the headmaster at the Emily Dickinson School—a private school on the Upper East Side. Very sound"—she nodded—"or I never would have sent my daughter there. Oh, here she is."

The girl walked straight over to me, said, "Mrs. Lambert, I'm Ramona Zarrow," and offered her hand.

I took it. "How do you do, Ramona? Why don't you bring over a chair?"

The girl rolled a redwood lounge next to me, set the back up straight, and lowered herself into it. She was three or four inches shorter than her mother, curved and graceful where her mother was angular and awkward, pretty where Edna was plain. She wore a black bikini, covered, more or less, with a blue denim work shirt tied below her round young breasts, buttons undone, sleeves rolled above the elbows. Her black, heavy hair hung loose almost to her waist. Her dark eyes were red-rimmed; her eyelids puffy.

"You know that Scotty was murdered," I said gently.

"Yes. Mother told me." Her voice was tremulous. "I wanted to talk to—to someone about him. About the date we were supposed to have last night."

"I'll pass along to Lieutenant Bell whatever you want me to."

She nodded, satisfied. "Scotty asked me to go with him to a party at Kip Rodgers' house in Fair Harbor. He said he'd come by for me about nine-fifteen. I expected him to be late on account of the storm. Only he didn't come at all!"

"But you went to the party anyway?"

She nodded. "After I waited for him a whole hour, until ten-fifteen. I told Mother to tell Scotty to meet me there, if he came by or called after I left. And then my father walked me over to Kip's house."

"Which way did you go?"

"Down Blueberry to Center. We stayed on Center all the way through Dunewood into Fair Harbor. Kip's house is on the other side of Fair Harbor, on the Walk past Broadway."

"Did you see anyone from Sharon's Landing on the way over?"

She shook her head.

"Or notice anything—any sounds or lights going on or off in anybody's house? Or a ferry at the dock?"

She shook her head again. "I'm sorry. To tell you the truth, I was thinking about something, and I didn't notice *anything*. Daddy asked me what time I was coming home, and I didn't even hear him. He was kind of annoyed."

"Did your father approve of Scotty?"

"Approve?" She looked blank for a moment. "Oh, you mean did he like him? I'm sure he did. Scotty was very polite to him—and Ivan was too; Ivan Ballou, the boy I went with last summer. Good manners mean a lot to my father. He's European, you know." She smiled fondly, showing lovely white teeth.

"Ramona," I said soberly, "think about it a moment and tell me if you believe Scotty was the kind of person who'd make a date and then break it without calling."

"I don't have to think about it, Mrs. Lambert. I *know*—knew—Scotty and it wasn't like him. If he had to change his plans, he would have called me. That's why I wanted to talk to the police! I'm sure he meant to keep our date! Only—" She broke off and put her face in her hands.

Only somebody shot him first, I finished silently—after he got the brownies from the Milgrims' kitchen counter and before he had a chance to pick up Ramona to take her to the party. If Ramona and I read him correctly.

"Ramona," I said gently, and she raised her head. "Had you ever gone out with Scotty before?"

"Not exactly." She sighed and straightened her back. "Last summer, when we rented your house, I was going with Ivan Ballou. Scotty was Millie Mortimer's boyfriend, and the four of us used to walk to Ocean Beach and things."

"Did you ever go to any of the bars?"

She shook her head. "Nobody was twenty-one. We went to the movies, mostly. The boys didn't have much money. Sometimes Millie and I bought us all pizza or ice cream cones. We had a lot of fun." She blinked and looked down at her hands. "I have to go to the john again." She stood up. "It's my contacts. When my eyes water a lot, the left lens slips down into the corner. I guess I'll have to go over to Bay Shore on Tuesday and get it adjusted."

She walked across the side deck and into the house again, through the back door. I watched her, and then I thought about the tall, stooped, unshaven man who had rushed past me on the dock that morning. He was the only passenger on the nine-thirty ferry back to the mainland; he must have been Helmut Zarrow.

"Edna," I said, "did your husband go home this morning or over to his sister's house?"

"Why? Why do you want to know?" The square jaw began to quiver again. . . .

"He walked through Sharon's Landing with your daughter Saturday night. Just after somebody committed a murder. The police will want to know whether he saw or heard anything."

"No," she said roughly. "I'm not going to let the police talk to him!"

"Edna . . ."

She dropped her head and picked at the hem of her tennis skirt with long, large-knuckled fingers. Then she raised her eyes and said, "Over there he was in the camps. He was just a child. His family all died in Belsen." She sighed. "Most of the time it's gone from his mind. But last fall, there was a robbery in his office; two men with guns came in and took everybody's money. Then the police came and asked everybody questions. They asked Helmut more questions than anybody because he was the office manager and a very responsible person. I *explained* that to him, but it didn't help. The nightmare started again. He's better, now, but if the police . . . ," her voice wandered off.

I thought about that a minute. "Maybe if I talked to him the police wouldn't have to."

She picked at her hem some more and considered the idea. "Well, he does like you; he told me so—even though he never met you and only talked to you on the phone. As soon as you and Ramona finish, I'll call him."

The girl had returned.

"Anything else I can tell you, Mrs. Lambert? I want to help!" she said earnestly.

"I was wondering," I asked, "when Scotty made the date with you."

She put her hands together and laced her fingers and looked down at the deck when she answered. "Around five. He'd just come off the court. He looked kind of grim." She swallowed and repeated, "Around five."

I didn't believe her. What a strange thing to lie about, I thought. What difference could it possibly make whether he asked her at five or at six?

Ramona unlaced her fingers and said, "I have to write to Ivan about Scotty. He's in Australia with his family."

"How about Millie Mortimer?" I asked. "Shouldn't somebody write to her too?"

"What makes you think I know where she is? She never gave me the slightest hint that she was going to duck out, in spite of what anybody thinks!"

"Anybody? Who, for example?"

"Mrs. Mortimer. She had the gall to come around and wait for me outside my school. 'Ramona,' she said, sweet as sugar, 'what have you heard from Millie?' When I told her Millie hadn't written to me at all, she dropped the sugar business and shouted at me like she was crazy. Can you imagine? Right in front of my school!"

15

THE STACCATO SOUND of a helicopter overhead is an ordinary occurrence on our island, nothing to get excited about. Sunbathers don't even bother to look up from their books or their Scrabble boards, knowing that it's the police again, in their trim blue bug, on their way to an emergency call in one of the big communities to the east—Ocean Beach, nine times out of ten. Or the Coast Guard scanning the water for a fishing boat that's run out of gas. Or an army or navy copter pilot putting in practice time. Occasionally, a sleek little private number hovers over the water just beyond the swimmers (one of them parks, every so often, among the cars in the ferry terminal lot on the mainland). And three or four times a summer, a ponderous white machine with New York Telephone insignia on its side settles on heavy pontoons in the ocean east of Sharon's Landing and then rises again, some mysterious mission accomplished.

Edna Zarrow stood over me wringing her hands when I picked up the phone to talk to her husband, but she moved to the windows and looked out when she heard the helicopter. I was glad it distracted her, but I didn't pay it any attention.

Helmut Zarrow said, "Hello, Mrs. Lambert," in a precise, lightly accented voice. "How does the ocean look?"

I laughed, as he meant me to. "The fog lifted, and the water's very blue and growing calm. Did I always ask you that?"

I heard him chuckle. "Yes. Every time." Then he said stiffly, "I was sorry to learn about the young man's death."

"We think he was shot just before you and your daughter walked over to Fair Harbor. If you saw anything unusual, we'd like you to tell us."

"For you," he replied, "I'm glad to be of assistance." He cleared his throat carefully and said, "Only one thing. When we came to Center, I heard a ferry start its engine. It was the *Firefly*, if I'm not mistaken. It was ready to pull out, for the captain turned on the big spotlight at the top of the wheelhouse and twisted it around the way they always do when it's dark, to see if they have to wait for someone running to catch the boat. The light went over Blueberry all the way up to Center."

"*Was* someone coming?" I asked, and when he paused before answering me, I noticed the rat-tat-tat of the helicopter again, circling, preparing to land on our beach.

"There were two men on the walk. One of them, the man who rents the Ballou house, was running for the ferry—the captain waited for him. The other man just stood there. When the light caught him, he raised his arm to cover his face and turned his head away from the bay, toward the tennis courts." Helmut cleared his throat again. "I think he didn't want anybody to recognize him. Of course that's just my impression. Perhaps he was startled by the light."

"Could you tell who it was?"

"Yes. The painter, Mr. Fry."

The helicopter circled slowly and settled on the sand just beyond the green swimming flag to the east of the lifeguard stand. Two policemen jumped out and raced to the beach stairs in time to help Harry Bell and Will Mortimer maneuver the steps with their makeshift stretcher and its occupant: Al Fry, in a robe and pajamas, his round body tilted backwards on a straight-backed kitchen chair. The little artist groaned as the men helped him into the copter.

Cissy, right behind them, carried his slippers. "I'm going along. Help me up," she commanded.

The dark-skinned policeman shook his head. "Sorry, lady. There's only room for three on this thing. We'll take good care of him."

"I'm going!" Cissy screamed. "He's my husband, and I'm going with him."

Harry interceded. "Let her take your place, Gomez. I'll be responsible. We'll keep you busy here."

I grabbed Will's arm. "What is it? What's the matter with him?"

"Appendicitis."

"Oh, God," I said, dismayed.

"He'll be all right, Lily. They'll have him at the hospital in five minutes; the surgeon's waiting for him. It could have been something worse."

"I know. I'm glad it's not his heart or anything. It's just that—"

"Move back, everybody." Gomez, the policeman, directed traffic. "They're ready to lift off."

We retreated with the crowd in the direction of the lifeguard stand.

"Over here." Will took my arm and led me to the foot of the beach stairs. Everyone was watching the copter. The rotors spun, raising a small sandstorm.

"I have to talk to you." Will's voice was low and urgent.

"When? Where can we go?"

He looked at his watch. "Leave your house in half an hour, at a quarter after twelve, and walk east on the beach. I'll catch up with you at that empty stretch just before Robbin's Rest. Caroline has a tennis game at noon."

The helicopter rose straight up, swung backward for an instant, and then surged over the dune and above my house toward the mainland. When it was out of sight, the Herb Rosens and their guests returned to their big red beach umbrella and picked up their books again. The MacKays went back to their Scrabble board. A small Jessup boy finished digging a moat around a sand castle; Ginger Van Buren put a bathing cap on and waded into the water, and two young men began throwing a bright orange Frisbee back and forth at the edge of the ocean. I climbed the beach stairs with Fred Mulloy and Harry.

16

SERGEANT BRADY MET us at the door. "Telephone, Lieutenant. The M.E." He smiled at me, his thick, sand-colored mustache turned up at the corners.

While Harry talked on one of the black phones on my card table, Fred sat at my round oak dining table and watched me grind coffee, fill the pot, and set out mugs and milk.

"Mind if I smoke, Mrs. Lambert?"

I answered by bringing him one of the ashtray-sized clam shells I had collected on my first walk by the ocean Friday evening.

Harry finished his call and came into the kitchen. "Coffee's ready. I can sure use some!" He filled the mugs.

"While you were at the Frys', I had visitors." I told them everything Ramona Zarrow had told me—except the bit about Caroline Mortimer making a scene in front of Ramona's school.

Then I asked, "Did Al Fry say anything?"

Harry shook his head. "He was so sick he could barely groan."

"Too bad," I said. "Helmut Zarrow saw him last night, walking toward the bay, on Blueberry, just before the ferry left, at 10:15. Al was *sick;* he should have been in bed—not wandering around outside. I sure wish we could talk to him."

Harry called Sergeant Brady to the kitchen counter, gave him some coffee, and said, "Phone Good Samaritan. Tell them to let us know when we can talk to Mr. Fry." He frowned, looking out at the sky—cloudless, pristine. "It would have been too much of a coincidence for him to fake a stomachache last night and come down with acute appendicitis today." He shook his head. "It's strange. I wonder what was important enough to get him out of bed and out of the house? Do you think it was murder? Can you imagine a man with appendicitis getting up and dressing and going down to the beach on a rainy night and shooting someone?"

He brought our coffee to the table and sat down with us. "What did you get, Fred?"

The young detective said, "Nobody I talked to admitted owning a gun or knowing anyone out here who had one." Then he pulled out a pile of tennis tags from his left-hand pocket, placed them on the table next to his coffee mug, and read their labels: "Borg. Van Buren. Huff. Girard. Milgrim (Esmée found them in a kitchen drawer). And Herbert Rosen. Two tags each." He brought out three more tags. "One tag each: Sonny Peabody. He found it hanging on his kitchen bulletin board. Arnold Rosen found his hooked into the pocket of an old work shirt, and Mr. Peter Raymond found his in a kitchen drawer. I gave receipts to the owners."

He consulted his notebook.

"Mrs. Jessup didn't have the slightest idea where her tags were, and I didn't ask her anything else because her children were crying, and she was cleaning up after the dog, who had vomited on the kitchen floor just before Mr. Jessup got him out of the house and down to the ferry to go to the vet on the mainland." He grinned. "Just like my house.

"Mr. Elmo Kesselbaum wouldn't let me in. I asked him, through the screen door, about the tags, but he didn't know what I was talking about. Claimed nobody ever gave him any—or, if they did, he dumped them in the garbage. Then he asked me to leave so he could get back to work.

"Mrs. d'Angelo threw out her tags two years ago when they remodeled the kitchen.

"The MacKays threw theirs away last fall, when they closed the house for the winter.

"That's all on the tags so far, except that I don't think having a couple of tags or not having them proves anything—except, maybe, the kind of housekeeper the missus is."

Harry pulled on his sideburn. "What else did you get?"

Fred looked down at his notebook again and cleared his throat.

"Mr. and Mrs. MacKay were the first people I saw, and they were very cooperative—for lawyers. Said they picked up the Frys at their house at about twenty to eight, stopped in Fair Harbor to buy wine for their party hosts, and then walked to Saltaire, arriving about a quarter to nine. They returned home on the lateral ferry at midnight with Mrs. Fry."

He consulted his notebook. "Next, I saw a lady named Fredericka Borg, with a beautiful voice. Every word comes out just so. Says she's a soap-opera actress in television. She was barefoot except for a sock on one foot; she cut it on a shell, she said, and apologized for not getting up. A guy half her age, name of Timothy Weed (says he's a set designer), got the tennis tags from the kitchen bulletin board. Saturday night, Borg and Weed went to Ocean Beach for dinner. Just before nine, they boarded the lateral ferry to come home. But it stayed right at the dock until the storm passed and didn't leave for Sharon's Landing until a quarter to ten, they thought. Neither of them had a watch, so they weren't sure. More about them later."

Fred continued. "Huff. Mr. and Mrs. Huff are in Italy

on a hiking trip, according to Mr. Huff's mother—who claims to be eighty-two, but who looks spry enough to me to be over there hiking herself. Matilda, the old lady, found the tags right away. She says she was alone in the house from eight-thirty on, when her granddaughter, Katie, went to baby-sit at the Girards, and she finished a game of chess," he raised his eyebrows, "with Sonny Peabody. She confessed to being frightened during the storm, but she said that Mrs. Lambert, here, came over at a quarter to ten and sat with her and gave her something to drink."

They looked at me, and I nodded. "I left about half an hour later."

"So she said." Fred grinned. "Matilda, the old lady, took quite a fancy to me. And I kind of liked her myself. She has this snooty accent, but that's only because she comes from London, England."

"And the Van Burens?"

The young detective scratched the back of his head. "Well, this sweet-faced lady lets me in. Black lady. She plays the flute with a symphony orchestra. And he writes operas, for God's sake. Soft-spoken people, about thirty, low-keyed—though he seemed a little skittish. They have a four-year-old daughter. They were supposed to go out to dinner with the Girards, but there was some problem because the regular sitter canceled at the last minute. So the Girards came over instead. About eight-thirty. They stayed until ten-thirty, quarter to eleven. Mr. Girard runs an art museum. How do you like that?"

"And now the Rosens. The Arnold Rosens." He consulted his notes. "Mr. Rosen's in TV—produces commercials, he says. Wife's a good-looking blonde, so skinny you can see her backbone from the front. Says she used to be a model before she had her kids and put on too much weight." He grinned. "Anyway, last night was their anniversary. The Herb Rosens and their guests—a couple from Baltimore—came over about eight with champagne and caviar."

He raised his eyebrows. "They were eating and drinking when the storm came and went. The eight of them (the Arnold Rosens have weekend guests, too) planned to go up to Cherry Grove on the lateral ferry to see the show at the Ice Palace. Because the Rosen house is right at the dock, they could wait in the living room until they saw a ferry turn into the channel and approach the dock. The lateral ferry was due at nine-fifty. But then minutes after the storm ended, somebody saw the *Isle of Fire* approaching. Everybody said it was too early to be the lateral, but the two Rosen brothers went down to the dock just to make sure. It was the regular ferry—the eight-thirty out of Bay Shore. Carl Hayes got off and then Dr. Mortimer, who talked for a moment with the two brothers and then said good night. A few minutes later, the *Firefly* pulled up; Arnold and Herb Rosen went out again to meet it. It was the lateral, all right, but it was going in the wrong direction—coming *from* Ocean Beach, where it had waited out the storm. The captain said he'd be heading east to Ocean Beach and on up to the Grove as soon as he'd made his run down to Kismet; he estimated half an hour. While the Rosen brothers were talking to the captain, Fredericka Borg hobbled off the boat, helped by that Weed fellow. At ten after ten, the group inside the Rosen house sighted the *Firefly* as it pulled out of Dunewood and headed into the channel. They all walked out on the dock. When the boat arrived, it was jammed with people from Fair Harbor and the other communities to the west, but the Rosen group were the only people from Sharon's Landing waiting to board. The deckhand closed the gate after them and then opened it again, for a straggler, who raced onto the dock.

Carl Hayes." He cleared his throat. "They arrived at Cherry Grove at a quarter to eleven and left at midnight."

"You're checking up on *everybody's* comings and goings?" I asked.

Fred nodded. "We are."

"Even people like—oh, like Brian MacKay or Ginger Van Buren who wouldn't have the slightest reason for killing Scotty?"

"How do you know?" Harry asked. "They might have some hidden motive."

"Such as?"

"Scotty might have been blackmailing them. Let's assume, for a minute, that Carl Hayes wasn't lying, that the idol of the kids really was a bum. Can you picture him as a blackmailer?"

"Well, he sure needed money," I admitted, "with graduate school ahead of him. And I guess he had plenty of chances to pick up secrets. The younger kids told him everything that went on at home. Older people confided in him too. He was a good listener—warm and caring. The kind of person who invited confidences, like Will Mortimer."

"So it's possible," Harry said. "You sure made a good case for it. But we don't have to worry about motives right now. I'm just trying to explain to you why we aren't ruling anyone out. At this point, all we're trying to find out is who had the *opportunity* to kill Scotty."

"You're working on the assumption that he was shot around ten o'clock?"

"Or a little before."

"And that the murderer intercepted him on his way to Ramona's house?"

"Right." He was drawing circles on his notebook with the inkless end of his pen.

"He must have intended to keep his date; he even

came back to the Milgrims' to pick up the brownies!" I frowned into my coffee. "But we can't be sure, Harry!"

He grinned. "Not yet. The autopsy shows his partially digested dinner—steak, potatoes, salad, blueberry pie—plus some food that wasn't digested at all. He ate some cheese within forty-five minutes of death, and ten or fifteen minutes later, he consumed a chocolate pecan brownie. We might find someone who saw Scotty eat the brownie or the cheese. That person might even have looked at his watch. It's not too much to expect." He turned to the sergeant, who was standing beside him. "What is it, Brady?"

"Ballistics wants to talk to you."

Harry pushed his chair back and walked over to the black phone.

Fred shook his head. "I was hoping it was news about Mr. and Mrs. Banks. The Albany police ran by their house and found it locked up. A neighbor said that they drove off with the little girl about a week ago. In their camper. Heading west, she believed."

"Paula Wohlens may know where they're going. Have you talked to her yet?"

He shook his head. "No answer at her apartment or her office. We even called Mr. Wohlens' office in Pennsylvania. Woke up the watchman. *He* gave us the secretary's home number. *She* was in church, but her mother said she'd have her call us." He grinned. "My call to Italy took less time."

"Italy! What in heaven's name for?"

"To track down Mr. and Mrs. Huff. They're staying in some tiny village up in the mountains, a couple of hours outside of Bolzano. But it only took five minutes to get Mr. Huff on the phone."

When Harry returned to the table, I said, "Scotty might have eaten the cheese when he was with Sonny Peabody. Let's see if Sonny's home."

The sergeant dialed the Peabody's number and we heard the phone ringing next door. Nobody answered.

"I'll leave him a note telling him we want to talk to him." I reached for my pad on the kitchen counter. "I'll drop it off at his house on my way to the beach. I'm going to take a walk. I need a little break," I said, as casually as I could manage. "I hope you can do without me for a while."

Harry said, "Will you be back by one-thirty or so?"

I nodded and asked what he had in mind.

"Lunch. Would you like to eat with me at the restaurant in Fair Harbor?"

"Sounds great." I stood up. "Thank you."

"Oh, before you go, Lily, I think you ought to know that our ballistics people looked at the bullet the M.E. dug out of Scotty's shoulder. It came from a .45."

17

IN A MOMENT of panic before I left to meet Will, I hid myself under a large straw hat, a pair of sunglasses, and a baggy beach jacket. It was a useless gesture. The first person who saw me—Edna Zarrow—pierced my disguise with a single, casual glance. She was standing on the bottom step of the beach stairs tucking her hair into a bathing cap covered with bobbing yellow rubber daisies. She grinned at me, thrusting out her horsy jaw, and whispered a conspiratorial, "Lily! Anything new?"

I shook my head vigorously and cast her the kind of remote smile that implied I'd come down to the beach on very, very important business. Then I hurried past her, praying hard that nobody else would notice me and ask the wrong questions, or come to the right conclusions. Thanks to the blazing noon sun, nobody did. As I made my way between striped beach umbrellas and prone bodies scattered around the lifeguard stand, no one looked up through the glare. Not even the lifeguard. His nose buried under a snowbank of Noxzema, he cowered in the shade of a towel draped over his head and squinted out at the black shapes of swimmers in the shimmering ocean.

With a sigh of relief, I turned east and headed up the beach. The tide was out, uncovering a flat field of sand, shiny-wet, mirroring the pale, gleaming sky, and ending in the flash of a tide pool. Beyond the pool was a naked sand bar and then the silver ocean. As I walked, a light, fresh breeze cooled my skin and warmed my blood.

Inch-deep tide puddles and rivulets still dotted the springy wet sand; I skirted the puddles, studying their residue of stone and tiny shells, and forded the rivulets, plunging in over my toes, splashing with abandon.

I hurried through Town Beach, packed with mainland familes streaming back and forth to the ocean and up and down the beach stairs to the toilets. Beyond the swimming flag and the Frisbee players and paddleball games, a group of youths drank beer and lounged on scruffy blankets. Twenty feet beyond them, a pair of young women settled themselves on low beach chairs and slathered suntan oil over bare breasts. Coolly nonchalant, they watched me pass; only their eyes betrayed a wary hostility.

And then the beach was empty. In the distant ocean, a lone surfer floated on his board, waiting for a high, free ride on a breaker. I stopped and took off my hat, watching him, waiting for Will.

He broke out of the crowd at Town Beach, jogged past the beer drinkers and bare-breasted sunbathers, hair ruffling in the breeze, legs flying, grinning when he caught up with me. Then he leaned down and kissed me on the mouth. I closed my eyes and pressed against him, wondering whether I could get him off the beach and into the bushes—at Robbin's Rest, perhaps, where the foliage was thick and the houses far apart.

I opened my eyes as two square, Germanic ladies, pursuing their consitutional in the undulating air, plodded toward us, frowning. Will straightened up and cleared his throat; with shaky hands, I put my hat back on.

When the ladies passed and we were alone again, walking up the beach, I asked, pressing my shoulder against his arm, "How's Al? Have you heard?"

Will put his arm around me. "His appendix is out, and

he'll be fine. The surgeon called just before I left the house." He shook his head. "But it was right down to the wire."

"When do you guess we could talk to him?"

"Around dinnertime." He dropped his arm and looked at me sharply. "Why? Do the police think he knows something?"

I nodded, and he frowned at the sand. "What about Caroline?" His voice was tight. "Does Lieutenant Bell think . . . Does he suspect her?"

"Do you?"

Will winced.

"I'm sorry," I said miserably. "That was a stupid thing to say." I touched his arm, trying to console us both. "Besides, Caroline isn't the only suspect. Carl Hayes had a fight with Scotty; Leo Milgrim wanted him out of the way, and the police are checking *everyone's* movements!"

"Thank God!" He smiled at me, so hopeful now, that I didn't have the heart to tell him what Harry told me about the bullet. "What about tonight? I'll come up to your house?"

I nodded, thinking about the bushes again. We were almost at Robbin's Rest. I was just about to reach for his hand when I heard a young woman's loud, angry voice.

"Get lost, Granny!" The speaker was facing us, and I could see extreme annoyance on her face. "Stop bugging us, you old fool!" She clutched at the beach towel wrapped around her body, tucked in, sarong-style, under one arm.

"Shut up, Brenda. Let me handle this." The man beside her wore a green-and-white striped towel where his bathing suit should have been, and he held the ends tightly together at his waist. "Now, Granny." He smiled—a conciliatory smile—at the stooped woman in rose-colored slacks and a straw beach hat whose back was to us. "Why don't you just walk on into Ocean Beach and tell the police there what's on your mind?"

The woman switched a white pocketbook from her left hand to her right. "Young man, I have made a find that is of utmost importance to the police. Now will you go and call them?"

Her voice was shaky, but the words were clear and clipped, the accent unmistakably British. Will and I grinned at each other and rushed into battle.

"What's the trouble, Matilda?" He drew himself up to his full six-foot-two. "Can we help you?"

"Oh, Dr. Mortimer!" Matilda put the accent on the "Doctor." "And Lily. I'm so glad to see you!" The small, even teeth in her dentures gleamed as she smiled, crinkling and creasing her flour-white face. "I found a gun."

"Where, Matilda?" I asked.

She pointed with her pocketbook to a black object sticking out of the edge of the tide pool.

"Would you call the police, Lily, while Dr. Mortimer and I keep watch over the gun? We don't want anyone to walk off with it. I know it's important to the police because Detective Mulloy asked me this morning if we had a gun in the house."

"Where's the nearest phone?" I asked Brenda.

"Use mine." She nodded toward a ramshackle house behind the dune and muttered, "Be my guest."

Five minutes later, Harry and Fred, with Gomez, the policeman, drove out across the wet sand and stopped where we were waiting. The black object sticking out of the sand by the tide pool was the gun handle. The barrel was buried in the sand. Fred dug it out and placed the gun on the hood of the patrol car. Then he turned to Matilda.

"What are you doing here, Mrs. Huff? How'd you get so far from home?"

"I was on my way to Ocean Beach."

"What?"

She glared at him. "Don't look so surprised, young man. I'm in perfectly good health, and I stroll up to Ocean Beach whenever I can. Whenever the weather's nice. It's very nice today, you'll notice." She nodded emphatically. "With the tide out, the walking is easy. There's a cool breeze, and I have my hat."

Harry shook his head. "How did you happen to notice the gun?"

"It was just good luck. That's all." She smiled. "I was moving along slowly, the way I always do, looking at the people on the beach. Just past Town Beach, I noticed a marvelous young man on a surfboard ride in on a long breaker. Then the beach was empty, and I didn't see anybody for a while, until way off in the distance I noticed a man and a woman. They were sitting on those chairs people use when they don't want to sit directly on the sand. Only they lowered the backs, and they were stretched out, sunbathing. The chairs lifted them off the ground a little, or I wouldn't have been able to tell, from far away, that they were both stark naked!" She straightened her back and sniffed with disapproval. "I was shocked, I have to admit. I read about nude sunbathers in the *Fire Island News*, but I never, well, stumbled on any before. I didn't want to look at them, so when I went past, I walked as far away as possible—all the way out here to the tide pool. I kept my eyes lowered, of course. Which is how I happened to see the gun." She shuddered. "For a moment, I thought it was a rock."

She smiled up at Fred. "You asked me this morning whether I owned a gun, so I knew you'd want to know I found one! But I didn't dare pick it up and put it in my pocketbook, and I didn't dare leave to locate a telephone. There wasn't another living soul in sight except the two—nudists, so I had to turn around and look at them, after all." She clutched her pocketbook against her chest. "I decided to look just at the *female*. I walked back to her and told her to call the police. She wouldn't do it." Matilda sighed. "She thought I was dotty."

I stared at the gun. "What kind is it?"

"Colt .45. An oldie." Harry traced with a forefinger the three ancient half-circles scratched on the handle to form a rainbow. He turned to Will. "Ever see it before?"

Will shook his head. "I suppose it's Caroline's."

"I suppose it is." Harry nodded slowly. "We'll ask her," he said, adding not unkindly, "before we do, Dr. Mortimer, you'd better get her a lawyer."

18

MATILDA TURNED DOWN Harry's offer of a lift. Will, unexpectedly, did too.

"I need the exercise." He pounded his fist into his palm. "And some time to think."

I watched him start down the beach, head lowered, shoulders slumping. Then I climbed into the back of the patrol car alongside Harry.

"The woman who hosted Caroline Mortimer's women's group." I thought for a moment. "E. J. Warner, right?"

Harry nodded.

"Have you talked to her yet?"

"No," he said. "Detective Mulloy is going to see her as soon as Gomez, here, can get him to Fair Harbor. Something special on your mind?"

"Have him ask her what Caroline Mortimer drank at the meeting, and how much."

"Why do you want to know?"

"Because if she were sober when she left Ms. Warner's house, she could have walked to Sharon's Landing on Center in about fifteen minutes."

Harry peered at me over the top of his glasses. "Thanks," he said.

"We're after the truth," I mumbled, "aren't we?"

He nodded and leaned forward to talk with Fred Mulloy, who was in the front seat.

We were approaching Sharon's Landing. Harry put his hand on my arm. "Stay put. Gomez is taking the gun over the causeway to the mainland. He'll drop us at the Broadway beach stairs on the way."

I had forgotten our lunch date.

The Fair Harbor beach stretches almost half a mile between Dunewood and Saltaire. Two sets of lifeguards watch over its swimmers, and three sets of beach stairs climb its dunes. The patrol car, its siren off, bumped slowly through the deep sand behind the sunbathers and let us off at the middle set of stairs. We climbed the steps to Broadway.

Unlike its city counterpart, Fair Harbor's Broadway is a residential thoroughfare for most of its length. Beach houses, up near the dune, balance on spindly locust posts high off the sand; halfway down to the bay, at Center, the foliage thickens. Sturdy Japanese pines and Russian olive bushes screen old, rectangular wooden cottages and their dark porches. Just before it crosses Bay Walk and merges with the approach to the dock, Broadway doubles its width, and the business district begins—the big, busy grocery; Unfriendly's, the ice-cream dispensary, cut out of the store; and, a few steps closer to the dock, the entrance to the restaurant. Around the corner, a general store (housewares, paperbacks, and clothing), the liquor store, and Fair Harbor's firehouse look out toward the bay.

Inside the grocery, lines of shoppers just off the beach waited by the three checkout counters. Outside, every parking space in the bicycle stand across the walk was taken; barefoot customers trod carefully around empty red wagons and bicycles leaning on their kickstands. Karen Rosen, long and lean as a swamp reed in a string bikini, stood by the newspapers stacked on the bench by the store entrance. She shifted her bag of groceries and said, "Hi," smiling her toothpaste-ad smile at the two of us, scratching the instep of one bare, bronzed foot with the heel of the other. Two boys filled a rubber raft at the grocery's air pump, its loud whine sounding above the roar of a motor boat just off the dock and the chatter of children waiting in line to buy cones. Harry wandered over past the air pump to a bulletin board, glanced through the sheaves of penciled notes offering to clean houses, repair bicycles, teach Yoga, tutor French, rent a sailboat, or sell an every-other-weekend share in a group rental, and wandered back.

"Sonny Peabody's here." I nodded toward a large red tricycle just beyond the line for ice cream. The fat boy sat on the saddle, his weight compressing its springs, his large rump overflowing its circumference. With glazed eyes and quick, greedy licks and bites, he was devouring a double-scoop cone, chocolate on top, pistachio on the bottom.

I introduced him to Harry. He nodded in acknowledgement, licking up the remnants of the chocolate scoop.

"I got your note, Mrs. Lambert, and I came over to your house, but you were gone." He ran his tongue around the top edge of the cone, capturing escaping drips of melted pistachio. "What do you want to know?"

"When Scotty was over at your house last night, did you give him anything to eat?"

He blinked in surprise. "Why do you want to know something like that?"

"Because it's important," I insisted.

"You and my mother!" He lowered the cone in disgust. "She yelled at me when she found out."

"Found out what?"

"That we ate the cheese. She called this morning and told me to take it to the Jessups'. They're supposed to have a party tonight, only now maybe they won't, on account of Scotty . . ." His voice wavered. "Anyhow, the cheese is mostly gone." He shrugged, tipped his head back, and sucked the rest of the ice cream into his mouth. "When the storm started and the lights went out,

139

Scotty and I lit candles and kind of hopped around at first, when the lightning was right overhead and flashing through all the windows at once. It was scary." He bit off a piece of cone and chewed it. "You know how it was."

I nodded.

"But when the storm started to move out over the ocean and it wasn't scary anymore, I got hungry and took a candle and looked in the refrigerator." He popped the bottom of the cone into his mouth and wiped his lips with the back of his hand. "There was this huge piece of cheese just sitting there. I asked Scotty if he wanted any, and he said yes, so I brought it out to the coffee table, and we sat on the couch watching the lightning on the water and cutting off hunks of cheese and eating it until the rain stopped and the lights went on again, and Scotty said he had to go pick up Ramona." He looked sheepish for a moment. "I didn't get much dinner; I took potluck with Mrs. Huff and Katie, and there was just this little bit of chicken and peas and an *apple* for dessert, for God sakes!" He shook his head. "We played chess, afterwards—Mrs. Huff plays a good game for an old lady—and my stomach rumbled the whole time! That's why I kept eating the cheese even after Scotty left. How was I supposed to know my Mother brought it from Zabar's for the party?"

Harry reached for the boy's fat, sticky hand and shook it solemnly. "Thank you, Sonny. You've been a great help."

"I have?" He looked at me, shrugged, and turning the handlebars south, pedaled up Broadway.

19

THE HEADWAITER, A young man in white jeans, a green tee shirt, and a short, sand-colored beard, led us to a table by the floor-to-ceiling windows that looked out to the dock across Bay Walk.

We both ordered flounder, a green salad, and coffee.

"Here's to Sonny Peabody," I said.

"To Sonny!" Harry clinked his water glass against mine. Then he placed his notebook on the table, took out a pen, and put on his glasses. "Scotty died between ten and a quarter past ten. He was shot, according to the medical examiner, fifteen minutes to half an hour before he died—that is, between nine-thirty and ten. But we can lop off five minutes, since it must have taken him at least that long to go back to the Milgrims', pick up the box of brownies, and get down to the beach. So there it is, Lily: the murderer pulled the trigger between nine-thirty-five and ten o'clock!"

He snapped open the rings of his notebook. "Now let's see how many of our forty suspects we can eliminate. Starting at the bay." He took out the bottom half of the map I'd drawn. "The Arnold Rosens." He tapped his pen on the light blue house facing the dock. "I had a talk with them, myself; the Herb Rosens were there too." His pen touched the pink house next door. "And both sets of house guests. I'm satisfied that no one in the group was out of sight of the others between nine-thirty and ten-ten, when they all boarded the lateral."

"When the lateral ferry arrived the first time, from

Ocean Beach, did anyone get off except Fredericka Borg?"

"Only Timothy what's-his-name."

"Weed. He's the third or fourth man she's brought out here. Each one was young enough to be her own son. Usually they're actors. Fredericka's an actress—and that's almost all anyone knows about her." I frowned, speculating. "She and her beau could have moseyed up to the beach from the ferry by ten. Easy as pie. Even though she had a cut foot."

Harry grinned. "Yes, they could have. But they didn't. They went straight to the d'Angelos' instead." He touched the tip of his pen to the yellow house on the corner of Blueberry and Center. "The d'Angelos invited them for bridge along with the Jessups."

"Six people for bridge?"

"D'Angelo intended to play chess with Bo Jessup and leave the three women at the bridge table with Timothy what's-his-name."

"Weed."

"Yeah. Well, the Jessups arrived just before the storm, and nobody played anything for a while. D'Angelo lit candles and fixed drinks while his wife sat with the twins and Jimmy Milgrim. When the lights came on again, the kids went back to bed. Fredericka Borg and her friend still hadn't arrived, so the men decided to play bridge with their wives after all. As Bo Jessup dealt out the first hand, June Milgrim knocked on the door, let herself in, apologized for her concern about her son, and went into the bedroom to see him. That was at twenty-five to ten, according to Ben d'Angelo, who was resetting the kitchen clock. June chatted with the three boys for five or ten minutes; then she came into the living room, accepted a drink, pulled up a chair, and watched the game over Sharon Jessup's shoulder. Just as June sat down, Ms. Borg and her boyfriend arrived. Mr. d'Angelo fixed drinks for them and set up the chess board. When both games were under way, June watched two or three more hands, finished her drink, and left—at ten-ten or a quarter after, we figure."

The waiter brought our salads and a basket of breadsticks. Harry helped himself to a breadstick and placed the tip of it on the cedar house behind the pink one the Herb Rosens were renting.

"The Girards," he said, "spent the evening with the Van Burens. It was supposed to have been the other way around, but Ginger Van Buren called at eight and asked them to come over, explaining that the sitter had just canceled."

"Ramona Zarrow was the sitter. And she didn't cancel until *eight*?"

Harry moved his breadstick down to the Frys' white house. "Between nine-forty and ten, your friend Cissy Fry was eating dinner in Saltaire at a front porch table with her hostess and the MacKays."

"That cuts our bayside suspects to one," I said. "Al Fry, nursing a bad stomachache and unaccounted for between nine o'clock and ten-fifteen. I wonder what he was doing when Helmut Zarrow saw him?" Which made me think about Ramona Zarrow. "Eight o'clock!" I frowned at the salad and pushed it aside. "I want to talk to Ramona again, without her mother around."

He nodded, wrote something in his notebook, and put away the bottom half of the map.

The waiter brought our flounder. Harry, leafing through his notebook, hardly noticed.

"Eat up," I urged. "You need your strength. You've only eliminated half the suspects!"

He laughed. We ate in silence then, enjoying the fresh, sweet fish and the view through our window. We looked across Bay Walk, beyond a strip of red carnations and a patch of dusty miller, to the backside of the old freight house—a square wood building, floated over on a barge from the mainland years ago. Beyond it, out of sight, was the slip where the ferries docked. A few feet to the left, where Bay Walk met Broadway, the main section of the Fair Harbor dock stretched into the water—twice as long as our dock, twice as wide, and ten times as busy.

A boat was due; the *Traveler*, I saw, was rounding the channel buoy out beyond Kismet. Twenty or thirty people waited on the dock with their luggage. When the ferry arrived, they'd walk east through a gate, cross in front of the freight house, and board the boat around on the other side of the slip.

Watching the ferry approach made me think about some of our suspects. "The people who left Sharon's Landing yesterday. Are they in the clear?"

Harry opened his notebook. "Mr. Raymond and Mr. Kesselbaum left for the mainland at nine-forty. Herb and Arnold Rosen saw them board the ferry. So they're in the clear. And so are Paula and John Wohlens. Mrs. MacKay went with Mr. Fry to the liquor store—next door, here—and she told us that she caught a glimpse of Mrs. Wohlens going through the gate to the eight-twenty-five boat from Fair Harbor in the middle of a group of teen-agers. The eight-twenty-five ferry arrived in Bay Shore at five of nine—just as all hell broke loose on the bay. For the next hour, the Coast Guard informs me, not a single water taxi or private boat stirred out of its moorings on the mainland; the open area, on the other side of those islands out there, was too rough. The large ferries could have made the trip, but as it happened, none did.

"And the Peabodys—Sonny's parents?"

"In the city. From eight to ten, they were at Lincoln Center with two other couples at something called Mostly Mozart—whatever that means!"

I grinned. "They throw in a little Bach or Haydn sometimes."

"Now who else was off-island, as the natives say? The writer's wife, Mrs. Raymond. Nine hundred people will vouch for her. She was making a speech at a dinner in Colorado Springs. Ten people will alibi Carl Hayes' wife—all relatives of her mother, who was celebrating her birthday with a barbecue in her backyard." He grinned. "That's eight more out of the way. We're getting down to the wire."

He opened his notebook and took out the top half of the map. I leaned across the table, studying it upside down, until I realized that somebody was hovering over us, and it wasn't the waiter. It was Taki Andreapolis.

"Detective Mulloy said you were here. I'm sorry to bother you." He smiled ruefully.

"Pull up a chair," Harry said. Taki sat down between us.

"How's Jimmy?" I asked.

"Coping. And angry, like the rest of us. Only Jimmy's angrier than we are because he thinks he knows who the murderer is. He says," Taki spoke slowly, choosing his words with care, "that he heard his stepfather and his mother arguing, and that his stepfather said he was damn well going to kill Scotty if she didn't get him out of the house. I thought you ought to know."

Harry pulled on a sideburn. "We'll keep it in mind."

"Thanks for telling us," I added.

He slid back his chair, rose abruptly, and left.

Neither of us spoke for a minute. Then Harry said, "A lot of people say 'I'll kill you' and don't mean it." He paused. "Well, to go on, Dr. and Mrs. Andreapolis had company for dinner—a colleague and his wife who have a place in Seaview. The four of them sat down to dinner at nine, just as the lights went out. They ate by candlelight. After the lights went back on, Dr. Andreapolis opened a fresh bottle of wine, so they didn't get around to dessert and coffee until almost ten-thirty. During the whole meal, nobody left the room."

He signaled the waiter for coffee, frowned, and pulled on a sideburn. "I was thinking about what Dr. Andreapolis said. I guess we need to talk with Jimmy Milgrim's stepfather."

"That's easy to arrange." I motioned to the dock. "He just arrived on the *Traveler*."

Leo Milgrim stood watching the passengers for the mainland as they walked through the gate to board the ferry. He looked, I thought, as if he wanted to go with them. When he finally pulled himself away, he was the last person to leave the dock. He carried no luggage, only an elegant leather briefcase—the hand-stitched, hand-rubbed kind that always makes me think of British ambassadors in bowler hats. He was dressed in well-cut jeans, good boating sneakers, and a silky navy windbreaker—Fire Island attire, but middle age costly—the gospel in beach wear according to Saks. A small-boned man, he was almost exactly my height. Blue-tinted bifocals guarded his eyes, but his head was unprotected, and a new sunburn spread up a high forehead into his scalp, where the springy, iron-gray hair had thinned to a few soft feathers.

I hurried out of the restaurant and stopped him, explaining who I was and how I knew who he was. He erased the misery from his lined face and gave me a very special smile—warm, bright, edged with just the right mixture of interest and reserve. I tried my best not to like him immediately; his juries, I imagine, had the same trouble.

"You know," he said as we walked back to the entrance of the restaurant, "I was actually on my way to your house! June suggested it when I called from the mainland. She thought I'd better avoid our place until Jimmy calmed down." His voice, as resonant and well-trained as an actor's, carried every nuance of feeling that he wanted it to. He smiled again, adding, with dry, mocking self-pity, "My stepson thinks I killed Scotty."

At our table by the window, he shook hands with Harry and pulled up the empty chair that Taki had vacated. He put his briefcase on the floor, propping it carelessly against the chair legs, took a sip of the coffee the waiter placed in front of him, and asked, "What can I do for you?" as graciously and generously as if he were sitting in his own office, and the Suffolk County Police, hat in hand, had come to him for assistance.

"This is just an informal discussion," Harry said awkwardly.

"I understand." Leo smiled faintly. "June told me Scotty was killed sometime last night. Would you like to know what I was doing then?"

Harry nodded, adding, "If you don't mind," with such deference that I winced.

Leo put his elbows on the edge of the table and laced his fingers. "On Friday, after I put June on the ferry, I flew to Chicago. When I returned, yesterday afternoon, I caught the five-fifty boat to Sharon's Landing. June met me at the dock." He unlaced his fingers and adjusted his glasses. "We walked home. I showered, had a drink in the living room with my wife while our housekeeper fixed dinner, and about seven-thirty sat down to eat. Jimmy and the d'Angelo twins had eaten earlier, my wife said." He looked blank for a moment. "With Scotty, I suppose, though she didn't mention him. After we finished, June walked the boys over to the d'Angelos', and I went upstairs to my study. I'm working on a brief." He caught Harry's eye, appealing to him as another professional, another perfectionist. Harry nodded sympathetically.

"A few minutes later, I heard June dash up the stairs and turn on the TV in our bedroom. She'd mentioned at dinner that there was something she wanted to see at 8:30. When the storm started and the lights went out, she came into the study, and I poured her a good stiff shot of brandy—that lightning even scared me! When the lights went back on and the rain stopped, she rushed out of the house again. Over to the d'Angelos'. To make sure her precious little boy wasn't upset." He made no effort to keep the sarcasm out of his voice. But he sighed and said, "I really should be more understanding. Jimmy was all she had for so many years. Anyway, I went back to my brief as soon as she left. Half an hour later, she put her head in the door to report that Jimmy was fine and that she'd stayed to watch some bridge. I quit work about eleven, and went to bed." He watched Harry write in his notebook. "What else can I tell you? June and I left Sharon's Landing this morning at five-thirty. In a seaplane. June's brother is in the army, on his way to Germany. He had a two-hour layover at Kennedy, and June went out to be with him. I had a client in from Los Angeles who required my presence at the Hilton. Not for long, thank God."

Harry pulled on a silvery sideburn. "Last night, after you finished dinner, did you happen to notice what time it was when you went upstairs?"

"About a quarter after eight."

"Did you leave your study at any time after that? Before you went in to bed, I mean?" Harry grinned rather foolishly, and I winced again.

Leo thought for a moment. "I went to the bathroom. The one in our bedroom. June was already in bed, so it must have been around eleven. But that's the only time I left my desk."

"Did you go downstairs?"

"No," he said irritably. "I just told you."

"Was your study door open or closed?"

"Open, I believe," he said slowly. "June left it open."

"Did you see anyone, besides your wife, during the evening?"

"No. My back was to the door."

"Did you hear anyone come in or go out?"

He shook his head. "No. When I work, I shut out everything else. I'm sorry." He looked rueful. "The only thing I remember hearing was the ocean banging and booming down the beach. It was making quite a racket after the storm, and the tide was coming in, I believe."

"But don't you think you could have heard someone come in the front door, if you were listening for him? If you wanted to see him?" Harry spoke blandly, and then waited, easy and relaxed, his head tilted a little. I didn't know how in the world he stayed calm.

When Leo did speak, there was more wry amusement than tension in his voice. "Look here, Lieutenant Bell. In spite of what you might have heard from the gossips down on the beach and up at the tennis courts, Scotty was *not* threatening my marriage!" He swallowed and looked out past the dock to the backside of the *Traveler*, deep in its own wake, heading for the mainland. "Of course," he added, "I wasn't what you'd call *happy* to have him live in my house. My wife and I had an argument about that. I lost the battle." He took a sip of coffee.

"But not the war?" Harry smiled blandly.

Leo studied him above the rim. He took another sip, set the cup down carefully in the saucer, and said slowly, "You're right. I didn't intend to lose the war. I was going to make Scotty an offer—large enough so he could afford to move in with some group renters in Fair Harbor and have a nice little profit for his trouble—but not so large that it would seem like a bribe. It was a delicate situation. I planned to stay out on the island through the rest

149

of the week so I could talk to him about it over the next few days. I was going to put it in terms of what would be best for *Jimmy*—even to invoking the name and authority of one of the child psychiatrists I consulted. I'd have pointed out that he'd still be teaching Jimmy at the bay beach and at the tennis courts, still coming up to have dinner sometimes, or to play chess with him. But he'd be Jimmy's *teacher* again, not a father-figure. Not a substitute for me. Scotty was an idealistic young man. I think he'd have understood."

Harry twirled his pen with his fingertips. "And if he didn't?"

Leo looked up at him sharply. "I'm a trial lawyer. A good one. I win my cases because I build them carefully, brick by brick. I don't rush into things; I reason—weigh consequences." He smiled at the two of us. "Now let's assume, for the moment, that I put aside the cautious habits of my last twenty-five years and didn't prepare *this* case the way I've always done. Let's assume that I planned my strategy carelessly, without marshaling my arguments, without testing to see how effective they'd be, how likely it was that Scotty would rise to the bait. Let's assume that I blurted out my offer to Scotty. And he said no." Leo let his fist drop on the table, to emphasize that ominous, awful "no." "Would I kill him—and turn him into a martyred hero in the eyes of my stepson? Or would I try again to persuade him to leave—fashion new arguments, find new inducements for him to say *yes*?"

Leo removed his glasses and wiped them carefully with his napkin, revealing damp brown eyes and heavy pouches under the lower lids.

"You have a point there. You have a point," Harry admitted. The he said abruptly, "Your housekeeper. What can you tell me about her?"

"Esmée." Leo grinned with pleasure (and relief perhaps). "A month or so before our marriage, we started looking around for a really competent woman to help out with Jimmy and give June a little more freedom. Out of the blue, my son's old baby nurse called to see if I could handle some legal matter for her. My son is in his twenties now; the nurse always kept in touch with my ex-wife. Anyway, I mentioned the kind of woman I was looking for, and she mentioned her cousin, who was the best children's nurse in the city and a terrific cook besides, and who was free, unexpectedly, beginning the next day. We met Esmée; we all liked each other. And—what can I say?—she's been a godsend! I don't know how we could have managed without her these past two years!"

"She makes a good salary?"

"You bet! She deserves it. She's a lovely woman; she adores Jimmy, and she cooks and bakes like a dream."

Which reminded me of something. "The brownies," I said. "Did you happen to notice a plateful of brownies on the kitchen counter?"

"I sure did," he said lightly. "Even sampled them."

"You did? Esmée said you never ate sweets. And that June didn't either."

"The part about June is correct. The part about me should be amended to read that I *try* never to eat sweets." He patted a perfectly flat stomach. "Especially not chocolate." He leaned across the table and said in a stage whisper, "I'm a chocoholic. One taste, and I'm off and running."

"How many brownies did you eat?"

"Only one, yer honor. I snuck it off the counter on my way upstairs after dinner. June was out with the boys. And Esmée had her back turned. I devoured it in the privacy of my study." Leo put his hands in his lap and lowered his eyes. When he looked up, his face was sober, and he asked, very quietly, "How was he killed?"

"Shot. And left to drown."

Leo winced. "Have you found the gun?"

"We think so."

"Let's assume," Leo said thoughtfully, "that you still think I killed him. How did I get the gun?"

"Scotty had it. You took it away from him."

Leo grinned. "Do you really think a man my size and age and physical condition could have wrestled a gun away from that—that jock?"

Harry's eyes narrowed. The deference had been a ploy and it was gone now. "Mr. Milgrim," he said, "from what I've seen, you could have talked him out of it!" Then he signaled the waiter and asked for the check.

20

WHEN WE LEFT the restaurant, Harry made a call from one of the phone booths outside the grocery. It was a long call; I read through every notice on the bulletin board before he finished.

He hung up, finally, and stuffed his notebook in his pocket. "Would you like to walk home by way of the bay? Ramona Zarrow's baby-sitting; she's going to the bay beach with the little Van Buren girl."

"Fine. Anything turn up?" I meant about Caroline, but I hoped he didn't know that—although I was almost sure he did.

"Nothing useful," he said carefully, avoiding my eyes.

We turned east onto Bay Walk, squeezing through a tangle of people and wagons and bicycles in front of the liquor store and circling the two fire trucks that sat in the sunshine on the concrete square in front of the firehouse. At the end of the block, where Bay crossed Oak, the concrete stopped and Bay turned into an old-fashioned wooden walkway meandering around the shoreline. It made for pleasant, slow strolling, and it cheered me, as it always does, to be close to the water. At Dunewood, we stopped while Harry took off his shoes and socks so we could walk across the sand beach; we paused again while he watched a man and woman clamming by the Dunewood float and beyond them, a line of Sunfish with bright, striped sails, tacking one after another around a channel marker.

"Look!" He pointed to the last sailboat. It keeled

sharply and capsized in the water. The safety boat sped to its side, but the two young boys, bobbing on the waves in their orange life jackets, righted the tiny vessel and scrambled on board without help.

We ambled on to Sharon's Landing, leaving the beach when Crescent Walk began. Harry leaned against the railing at the Frys' ramp and wiped the sand off his feet. He looked so relaxed, with his bare feet and his sunburned nose, and so friendly, smiling his off-duty smile, that I forgot myself.

"Will you come out again," I asked impulsively, "when this is all over? When my brother George is here, and the three of us can have a long visit?" I swallowed and managed to mumble, "with your family, of course."

He froze; a barefoot statue. I held my breath until he thawed, pulled on his socks and slipped into his loafers. Then he said slowly and carefully, his eyes on the sailboats, "I'd like to come back some weekend. Maybe with my son. He's fifteen." He looked at me finally, his face a mask. "My wife and I are divorced." Then he rose and went to work. Turning his back on the bay, he stared at the Frys' house a long time. "Think with me a minute, Lily! About Al Fry. Does it seem likely—or even possible—that a little round middle-aged man with a stomachache could have disarmed a strong young man like Scotty and shot him?"

"It's possible," I said slowly. "Just barely. Al's agile, in spite of his weight; you ought to see him scurry around on his boat or track a bird in the wetlands out there." I nodded toward the long, empty bay island to the east. "But he looks as if he couldn't move quickly—and that might have thrown Scotty off guard." I sighed. "Still, it would be a lot easier to imagine him doing the shooting if he'd gone to meet Scotty with the gun in his hand."

He rubbed his chin, speculating. "What about Carl Hayes as our killer?"

"I don't know." I frowned at the sidewalk. "Carl could have taken the gun away from Scotty without a bit of trouble; and I can picture him pulling the trigger. In cold blood. Without the slightest provocation." I shuddered. "I want him to be the murderer, Harry! Only I don't think he did it. I can't tell you why, exactly. I guess it has something to do with that cock-and-bull story he told us about seeing Scotty in Ocean Beach on Saturday night, and then saying no, it was Friday."

"And Leo Milgrim? Can you picture him persuading Scotty to hand over the gun?"

I didn't have to ponder that one. "Easy."

"You think Leo shot him, don't you?" He tilted his head, half-grinning, as if he didn't believe it.

I hedged a little. "Leo might have shot him in a moment of anger or hatred or frustration. I could like the man, I confess, and I think he has a remarkably good mind. But just because he reasons well doesn't mean he's going to act any more reasonably under really terrible pressure than the rest of us. For my money, he's the best suspect we've got!"

Harry studied the tassels of his loafers. "Maybe we have a better one."

Before he had a chance to explain, Ramona Zarrow, pulling a wagon behind her, turned the corner onto Crescent Walk.

Ramona moved slowly—in order not to bounce around her small passenger—her body bent forward, her long black hair falling over the front of her denim work shirt, her eyes on the cement walk under her bare feet.

She stopped in front of Arnold Rosen's light blue house and glanced down at the beach, pushing the hair back from her face. "Patti and her mommy are here." She smiled affectionately at the child. "You can get out now, Mrs. Muffin Man." Toby Van Buren slung her chocolate legs over the side of the wagon. "But wait for me." She parked the wagon in the sand by the walk, scooped up the beach towels and tote bag, and took the small brown hand Toby held out to her. She wouldn't even have noticed us if Toby hadn't.

"Ramona's going to take me swimming," the child announced.

Ramona started when she saw us. Then she swallowed carefully. "Let me ask Mrs. Girard if she can watch Toby for a few minutes. While I talk to you."

She walked Toby across the sand to Suzanne Girard and her daughter. Watching her, I thought about all the sitters and au pair girls I'd observed on the beach and by sandboxes in the city parks when my girls and Woody were little. I used to grade their performances. Ramona's would have rated an A plus.

"Let's sit on the Frys' deck," I said to Harry. "Cissy won't mind."

When Ramona joined us, perching stiffly on the edge of a chair, Harry nodded to me, and I said, "You like to work with children?"

"Yes. Especially Toby." She rubbed a damp palm back and forth on her thigh.

"We understand that you were supposed to sit with her last night, only you canceled. At the last minute. At eight o'clock—even though you told me that Scotty made the date with you at five."

She sighed and hung her head and mumbled into her lap, "I didn't tell you the truth. I couldn't. Not with my mother there."

"Your mother's not here now, Ramona," Harry said, very kindly.

She sniffed and wiped her eyes with the tips of her fingers and told us exactly what I didn't want to hear:

"It was true," Ramona began, "about my seeing Scotty at five o'clock, right after he came off the court. Mrs. Milgrim hassled him, and he was plenty mad at her.

I just listened to him complain, and then after a while I told him that I had to baby-sit at 8:30, but that I'd be home from six o'clock on, holding down the fort while my folks were in Ocean Beach at a cocktail party." She sighed. "It was a pretty direct invitation. And strictly against the rules. My father's old-fashioned. He'll kill me if he ever finds out I invited a boy into our house when nobody was there! Anyway, Scotty turned up."

"When?" Harry asked.

"A little past six-thirty. He stayed for a couple of hours. We sat in the living room and talked, like old times, and listened to some records and, well, one thing kind of led to another, and when he asked me to go to the party with him, I just couldn't say no—even though I had to call Mrs. Van Buren at the last minute and tell her I wasn't going to sit for Toby!"

So far, so good. I had no reason to think it wouldn't continue that way. So I wasn't being obtuse when I asked her, "Where did you and Scotty go?" I was sure she'd say they went out for a stroll. Down to the tennis courts most likely, where he could have left her sitting alone on the bench for a few minutes—long enough for him to cross Center Walk, find nobody home at the Mortimers', and snitch the gun. He might even have *explained* that he needed to talk to Dr. or Mrs. Mortimer on some private matter. Which would tighten the noose around Leo Milgrim's neck (or Carl's or Al Fry's), put Caroline in the clear, and let Will off the hook so that we—

"I told you where we went!" Ramona's voice rose. "We went into the living room!" Her face turned gray under her tan, and she added, so softly I could barely hear her, "After a while, we went in my bedroom, but we didn't—"

"That's all right," Harry said. "Did you see where he went when he left your house?"

"Right across Ocean Walk to Mrs. Huff's. Sonny Peabody was waiting for him at the Huffs'."

Harry rephrased my question. "Did either of you leave the house at any time between six-thirty and eight-thirty?"

She shook her head.

"But he must have left," I insisted. "Maybe when you were taking a shower."

"I didn't take a shower!" Ramona's lower lip began to tremble. "I didn't need to take one! I told you. We didn't do anything!" She started to cry, and then caught herself. "He never left the house. Not for a minute. Please don't tell my father!" She covered her face with her hands.

From where we sat, on the Frys' front deck, we could see Ramona trudge through the sand to the edge of the water, lean over, and give Toby a kiss on the top of her head.

"Scotty didn't have a chance to take the gun. So that's that. Leo Milgrim didn't kill Scotty." I aimed for a light, Mozartian tone. It came out sounding like Wagner.

"Neither did Carl Hayes." Harry gazed at a trio of clammers making waves just beyond Al's boat. "Or Al Fry." He spoke as cautiously and as kindly as if he were paying a condolence call.

"Are you trying to break the news to me that we're back to Caroline Mortimer?"

He shook his head. "She's in the clear. She didn't leave Ms. Warner's house until five of ten. That's when Ms. Warner reset the clock on her stove. And you were right about her being sober. She didn't take a single drink all night, not even a glass of wine. She never does at these meetings, Ms. Warner said. Detective Mulloy is checking this with a woman on Elm Walk who sat next to Mrs. Mortimer all during the meeting and double-checking the time with a woman from Lonelyville who helped Mrs. Mortimer clean up."

"Is *anybody* left?"

"Only one, Lily."

I knew. He meant Will.

"He could have found the gun sometime after he came in from clamming and six-fifteen, when he left for the ferry. His wife was in the kitchen the whole time, you remember, fixing herself some coffee and preparing the stuffing for the clams. He showered, and when he finished, he went into their bedroom to dress. I don't know whether he slept in the same room with her, but he kept his clothes there."

I felt my face break up, and he paused and looked away while I pulled it back together.

"Caroline left her father's file, with the gun in it, right on top of their bureau. He was curious, I suppose, and he might have lifted the top. When he saw the gun, he could have decided to come back and get it before his meeting with Scotty."

It hurt to open my mouth, but I managed to ask, "And his motive? The same as hers?"

"Possibly. But Scotty may have been blackmailing him. When he went to the mainland last evening, he had dinner at the Surf Club with a woman. The wife of one of his patients, he said. But he had met her there at least twice before, and the two of them appeared to be, well intimate—according to the bartender at the restaurant. He knows Dr. Mortimer; the good doctor once took a shard of glass out of his hand."

I stood up and paced on the wooden deck, thinking as hard as I could under the circumstances.

"Look here, Harry," I said finally, "maybe he's the kind of man who always has to have a woman on the side." I took a deep breath and added grimly, "Maybe I mean a lot less to him than I thought I did. But he's a good, kind man! People always bring him their problems—along with their busted arms and cut feet. He isn't a killer! Will Mortimer didn't murder Scotty, I'm sure of it! We've overlooked something. We've made a mistake."

"What kind of mistake, Lily?"

"I don't know. Maybe about Carl. I think that horrible man is hiding something."

"Don't count on it," he warned. "But I'll talk to him again, I promise you, before we do anything else."

At that moment, the first siren went off.

21

IT'S A FIRE DRILL, I thought. *We're having a fire drill.*

"Look!" Harry pointed to a spiral of smoke rising over the pine trees on the south side of the tennis court.

The siren sounded again, urgent, insistent, echoed by the Fair Harbor siren half an octave lower.

We ran up Blueberry—just ahead of the Rosen brothers, their wives, children, and guests, the d'Angelo twins, and Sonny Peabody, pedaling furiously on his mother's trike. As we turned east on Center, Harry, in the lead, stopped suddenly in front of Fredericka Borg's side deck. Next door, at the Ballou house, black smoke poured out of the open glass doors in the living room.

"Stay here, Lily. You're barefoot," he said and raced to the hydrant by the tennis-court gate to help Brian and Jo-Ellen MacKay, who were struggling to hook up the hose.

I heard the crackle of flames and felt a rush of heat and motioned everyone to move back.

Brian opened the hose nozzle and shot a stream of water into the house. The smoke, retreating for a moment, rose again, paler, thinner, a little subdued. Moving closer, he angled the nozzle to his left and flooded the front part of the living room. The smoke turned white, and the crackle changed to the sizzle of steam.

Clanging its bell, the Fair Harbor fire truck approached from Dunewood, bouncing over the broken cement on Center Walk. Everyone turned around to watch it—everyone except me. I was looking at Fredericka Borg, limping back and forth from one end of her deck to the other in an organdy peignoir (lace-trimmed at the wrists and neckline) as out of place on our blue-jeans beach as a formal ball gown. But Fredericka's feet were pure Fire Island; the right one was bare; on her left foot she wore a thick white tennis sock to keep the sand from irritating the cut on the bottom.

Since I didn't turn around when everyone else did, I was facing the right direction to see the windows in the back of the Ballou house, and to notice the window farthest from the walk open slowly, just a little, just enough for a hand to reach through and drop a package, the size of an unopened steamer clam, into the thick, leafy patch of poison ivy below.

"Out of the way!" Sonny shepherded all of us into Fredericka's sandy yard, pulling the trike along. The fire truck passed, and the crowd surged back onto the walk.

"There's Carl!" Fredericka shrieked.

Carl Hayes pulled himself through a casement window and crawled out on top of a shed attached to the house on the south deck. If he'd had the sense to squat and let himself down easy, he wouldn't have been in any trouble, for it was only about four feet to the deck. But he stood up straight and jumped. The shed blocked my view, but I heard him howl with pain.

"What happened?" I called to Fredericka.

"He landed wrong. Did something to his ankle. Will Mortimer's coming."

The fire was out. Brian and Harry Bell turned off the hose, and the Fair Harbor firemen, who hadn't even unfurled theirs, went into the house by the front door. A moment later, they tossed out two sofa cushions, charred and soaked with water.

Sonny pulled the trike out of the sand, deposited himself on the seat, and pedaled slowly toward the Ballou house. I walked along beside him, thinking something about Sonny on the trike looked odd and trying to figure out why. Not odd, exactly. Different. He got off the trike where the Fair Harbor fire truck blocked the walk, and the two of us pushed it through the sand and back onto Beach Plum at the corner by the Mortimers' house. As he mounted the trike again, he caught me staring at him and blushed.

"What's the matter, Mrs. Lambert? Did I do something wrong?"

"It's not you, Sonny. It's your three-wheeler. When Lieutenant Bell and I talked to you in front of the store a couple of hours ago, I'd swear you were sitting on a red tricycle." I put my hand on the blue front fender.

"This blue one is my mom's. The red one belongs to Mrs. Wohlens. Right after I talked to you, I rode it up here. Frank asked me to. He found it sitting in front of his store last night, and he pulled it in out of the rain. He thought the owner would come back for it today, but nobody came, and he didn't know who it belonged to. I told him Mrs. Wohlens—there's a W scratched on the back fender—and he tried to phone her, but nobody answered. So I said I'd ride it home for her and put it in the shed under her house."

"You mean she just left it there and never came back for it? Why would she do that?"

He shrugged. "Maybe Mr. Wohlens—"

"He never rides it. He has his own bicycle. He wouldn't dream of riding a three-wheeler! Did Frank say when he found it?"

"Last night. He—"

"What time last night? What time? Did he tell you?"

"No. I'm sorry." With great care, Sonny placed his rump on the trike's saddle; the seat sank slowly. "Why don't you ask him?"

"I will," I muttered, scowling at the walk. "I will."

Brian MacKay said, "Excuse me, Lily. We need to get

by. Excuse me." He said it louder the second time, and I looked up and moved off Beach Plum into the sand by the Mortimers' bike stand. The Fair Harbor fire truck had gone, I noticed, and most of the fire-watchers. I frowned at the sandy yard, fretting about the red trike and Paula and John and Scotty.

Somebody cleared his throat.

I raised my head. Harry Bell was leaning against the bicycle stand.

"Are you okay?"

"Fine. Fine." I forced myself to focus on his face. "Just thinking."

He waited for me to explain. When I didn't, he said, "Carl Hayes is a lucky fool! He was sound asleep in a back bedroom with the door shut when the fire started. If the MacKays hadn't walked by when they did, the house would have burned to the ground with him in it. Lily!" Harry pursed his lips in exasperation. "Did you hear anything I said?"

"Of course. Every word. Why didn't the dog bark?"

"Because it wasn't there. It ran out of the house this morning and didn't come back. The dogcatcher found it in Kismet and took it to the pound. You know what started the fire? Carl left an ashtray on the arm of the sofa. He thinks he knocked it over on his way to the bedroom. Lily!"

"I'm listening! What are you going to do with him?"

"Nothing. Leave him sitting up there on his deck until it's time to put him on the 4:30 ferry. We would have sent him to the hospital in a helicopter, but he refused to go; he's terrified of flying." Harry pursed his lips in distaste. "A squad car will take him down to the dock, and one of his in-laws is going to meet the boat and drive him to the hospital. According to your friend, Dr. Mortimer, he may have broken his ankle." Harry folded his arms across his chest and looked uncomfortable. "After he finished with Carl, I asked Dr. Mortimer to come up to your house to answer some questions. He's there now, with Fred Mulloy, waiting for me."

"But you said you were going to talk to Carl, first, before—"

"I talked to him already."

"What did he tell you?"

"Nothing useful. Though he finally admitted he never saw Scotty in Ocean Beach—drunk or sober, on Friday or Saturday or any other night. When we asked him why he lied to us, he squirmed a little and muttered that he was just trying to make the big hero look bad."

I started. "Were those his exact words?"

Harry nodded.

"Do me a favor, will you? Tell Will I had to borrow Caroline's bike." I rolled it out of the stand.

"Where do you think you're going?"

"I need to check on something. I'll tell you all about it as soon as I can. I've found a new suspect."

"I bet you have," he said roughly.

Caroline's bike was a mess—handlebars askew, pedals crying for oil, tires gasping for air. But the bell worked, and I leaned on it, forcing strollers and small children into the sand and breaking up a group of people caucusing on the corner of Center and Broadway. I made it to the store in ten minutes; on her three-wheeler, which is slower and hard to maneuver, it would have taken Paula fifteen minutes, maybe a little more. I can walk to the store in twenty-five minutes, if I really push.

I parked in the last open slot in the bike rack and found Frank, watching over his gold mine from a post by the dairy counter and listening to a customer talk about Greek food. I caught Frank's eye, and he motioned for me to wait.

The customer, a leathery little man hugging a bag of groceries, went on and on.

"You're right," Frank encouraged, fawning all over him. "It's the oil that matters."

I shifted from one foot to the other, sighing loudly, and worried what Harry and Will were saying to each other. It was already three o'clock.

Finally the customer left.

"Do you know who that is?" Frank's voice was hushed, awed. "He's the biggest—"

"Listen, Frank. I need some information."

His pleasant Irish face sobered instantly. "For the police?"

I nodded. "About the trike that Paula Wohlens left in front of your store."

He raised his eyebrows. "I don't see—"

"I'll explain later. Just tell me when you first saw it— when you first noticed it."

"Before the storm."

"What time? I need to find out what time it was when she rode down here."

He frowned and rubbed the stubble on his chin.

"Last night. We were so busy here, I don't—wait a minute! Last night, I was in the store the whole time except when I went down to the ferry dock to see off my cousins and their kids, who'd spent the day on the beach. I visited with them for about five minutes—the ferry was packed to the gills—and then I left. The captain had just started his engine."

"What ferry was it?"

"The eight-twenty-five. When I came back to the store, I saw some customer had left a trike sitting there, right in front of the entrance, about five or six feet out. I moved it off to the side so that none of the other customers would trip over it. Everybody was rushing to get in and out before the storm, as you can imagine. At five of nine, when everyone was gone, the trike was still there, so I pulled it inside, where we keep the delivery boys' bicycles—those trikes are expensive, you know—and then I forgot about it this morning. The people on the mainland who deliver our Sunday *New York Times* had some kind of problem and only sent us about a quarter of the papers we ordered; I spent half the day explaining this to a couple of hundred customers who had to make do without their Sunday crossword puzzle until the missing papers turned up at noon. Anyway, I finally remembered the trike and brought it out front and asked Sonny Peabody if he knew who it belonged to. He told me it was Paula's; I tried to call her, but there wasn't any answer, and Sonny said he'd ride it back to her house." He paused and scratched his head and covered a yawn. "Strange, isn't it? I figured that some absent-minded customer met a friend in the store and started talking and walked home with the friend, forgetting that shc'd ridden here on her trike. Only that's not what happened at all. Paula parked her trike in front of the store and then left Fire Island."

"How do you know that?"

"I saw her board the ferry."

"With John? Was John with her?"

"I didn't see him," Frank said, "but there was a big crowd boarding; he was probably up ahead."

22

IT WAS LATER than I wanted it to be when I left the store, but I didn't hurry because I had some things to work out. There was a remote chance, I admitted, pedaling slowly up Broadway, that an unknown person borrowed or stole Paula's three-wheeler for a reason unconnected with the murder. But I put aside that possibility; I didn't even allow myself to consider it. I needed a new suspect in the worst way, and the more I thought about it, the more certain I was that John Wohlens killed Scotty and used Paula to give himself an alibi. He never left on the eight-twenty-five ferry, but he wanted us to think he did. So he made sure that Paula caught it. The hardest part of his plan was persuading her to help him without telling her too much. It couldn't have been easy. My guess was he told her part of the truth: perhaps that he had an appointment that was kind of delicate that he didn't want anybody to know about. When she finally agreed, it must have been so late that she had to ride the three-wheeler to Fair Harbor; she would have missed the boat if she had tried to walk. John didn't dare go after the trike, of course, but he didn't need to; he could always claim that someone stole it.

I glanced at my watch, pedaled a little faster, and put the rest of the pieces together. John killed Scotty because Scotty was trying to blackmail him. The two men came from the same town; their families knew each other; and Scotty was trying to cash in on some information he picked up back home that could have cost John his appointment as a college president. Afterwards, after he killed Scotty, he hiked up to Ocean Beach—or to Cherry Grove, perhaps, where the chances were even better that nobody on the ferry would know him—and caught a late boat to the mainland. He would have arranged for Paula to pick him up on a side street near the terminal. And while they drove back to the city, he must have told her what he wanted her to believe—that Scotty had a gun and threatened to kill him, and that he shot Scotty by accident, struggling with him over the gun. Paula would have promised to protect him, of course, to lie for him, to tell the police that both of them had left together on the eight-twenty-five ferry.

Everything fit, I told myself, basking shamelessly in self-approval as I pedaled through Dunewood. I needed evidence, of course, enough to convince Harry to forget about Will—but I was sure I'd come up with something when I searched the Wohlens' house, or when I talked to Carl, who knew more about the murder, I figured, than Harry thought he did. This time, Carl would tell me what he had really seen last night. He'd be forced to; I planned to blackmail him.

Center was deserted now, so quiet I could hear the *thwap* of balls through the trees next to the courts and the low rumble of the ocean. I parked Caroline's bike at the side of the walk by the back of the Ballou house and made my way slowly, gingerly, through reeds and clumps of dune grass and prickly bushes to the blanket of poison ivy leaves. If I'd been wearing sneakers and socks, I would have stomped around until I found what I was looking for. For a moment, I considered doing it anyway, and then I saw a long stick under the house and poked around with that. It shouldn't have been hard to find a white package the size of an unopened chowder clam, but all I turned up was a tennis ball.

"Lily! What the hell are you doing?"

I started and dropped the stick and stared in dismay at Paula Wohlens on the walk.

"What the hell are you doing?" she repeated crossly.

"Looking for a tennis ball. A brand new one," I said defensively. "Here it is." I plunged my hand into the poison ivy, picked up a yellow Wilson heavy duty, and waded out to the walk. "I hit it over the fence this morning five minutes after I opened the can." I tucked the ball into my back pocket. "Don't worry about my hand," I wiped it on the seat of my pants. "I never catch poison ivy. Where did you come from?"

"The three-fifteen ferry." She pushed her dark glasses onto the top of her head and rubbed her eyes.

Why did he send her back? I wondered. To cover up something? To find out what we knew?

"Where's John?" I asked cautiously.

"On his way to Philadelphia. I dropped him off at Penn Station. The people he's meeting there are going to drive him up to the college in a day or so."

"Did you hear about—"

"Yes." She bowed her head. "Bo told me. We came over together on the ferry." She sucked in her breath. "How can Scotty be dead?" Her voice broke, and she rubbed her eyes again. They were bloodshot and deeply circled, and the lids were red and swollen.

Poor woman, I thought. How terrible it is for her!

She picked up her tote from the sidewalk. "I hear you're helping the dicks. I don't suppose they've found anything?"

"Not really," I lied.

"I can't imagine anyone having a reason to kill Scotty."

Oh can't you, I thought bitterly, and walked alongside her, pushing Caroline's bike.

She watched me slide the bike into its slot in the

Mortimers' new rack, and as we started up Beach Plum, she stared at the charred sofa cushions propped against the Ballous' garbage shed and the smoke-stained wall on the living room. "What's this?"

I told her. "The renter survived, unfortunately." I nodded toward the big south deck where Carl, stretched out on a redwood lounge with the back propped up, was talking to a man in a black uniform. The fire warden.

Paula said, "I have to change. Bo talked me into playing tennis at four. With Edna and Sharon. To calm down Sharon, he claimed." She sniffed and wiped her nose with the back of her hand. "How can I play tennis?"

"You'll manage," I said roughly. Her deceptions—and mine—were getting me down. "May I wash at your house? I've never caught poison ivy, but I guess I shouldn't push my luck."

She nodded, and I followed her to the foot of her ramp, where she paused to retrieve an empty garbage can lying on its side in a bed of pink begonias, where the garbage man had dropped it. She put the top back on and placed it next to its mate, which stood covered and closed in the three-sided garbage shed. Then she hurried up the ramp, took the key out of her tote, and unlocked the front door. I saw that if she hadn't come back, I'd have been forced to break into her house, which I hadn't counted on doing. I had expected to find the key hanging on a nail under the eaves—where they always left it.

The kitchen and the living room looked neat enough; there were no signs that anyone left in a hurry. But the air in the house was stale and humid and smelled of ammonia.

Paula opened the sliding-glass doors that faced the walk and Elmo Kesselbaum's house. "That's better," she said, as a fresh breeze wafted in. She waved me into the big guest bathroom. "There's brown soap in the medicine cabinet. You'd better use it."

Paula's guest bathroom, like all the others in your basic Sharon's Landing house, had two doors. The one that opened into the bedroom hallway I left open. The other, which led outside to the back deck, I unlocked, as soon as Paula went into her bedroom and closed the door behind her. Then I took out the brown soap, which was soggy from sitting in some water on the medicine-cabinet shelf, and scrubbed my hands. I was drying them when she appeared in the hallway, barefoot, carrying sneakers and socks and her racquet and tote bag. She was wearing a white shirt and matching tennis skirt so new she had to tear the store ticket from the waistband.

"Nice outfit," I said as we walked into the living room. "Now you can put that tennis dress in the ragbag."

She smiled. "Maybe I will." Seating herself on the couch, she pulled on her socks and sneakers, tied the laces, and stood up. "I have to go." She rubbed her eyes again; they seemed to be bothering her a lot. "Why don't you come back and have a drink, Lily? About five-thirty. You can tell me what the dicks have turned up." She grinned, showing she was just curious; it was only natural to be curious; everybody was.

I shrugged and said, "There's very little to tell. But I'll take that drink."

None of us ever lock our houses when we're out here on the weekend, but Paula shut the sliding-glass doors and slipped the night-locks in place and adjusted the button on the inside doorknob so that when she closed the front door behind us, it locked automatically. "I'm scared." She shivered a little. "I don't want to come back from the courts and find a killer in here."

She left me at the foot of her ramp and strode down the walk just ahead of the fire warden, who paused at the burned-out sofa cushions to write something in his note-book, and then walked around the corner to Center.

Carl was alone. There wasn't time to look for the white packet again before the police came to take him to the ferry. I'll bluff it, I told myself, and climbed the Ballou's ramp.

23

CARL WAS DOZING on the redwood lounge, his left leg resting on a plateau of seat cushions from the redwood chairs.

I looked down at him for a moment. He was snoring lightly, and he smelled of stale beer. "Wake up," I said. "We have to talk."

He opened his eyes, and then closed them again and pretended I wasn't there.

"About a package. The one you tossed out the window when you thought the house was burning down."

He started so violently that his foot moved. He blanched and grabbed his knee, squeezing it, swearing through clenched teeth until the pain subsided. The he propped himself up on an elbow and invited me to do a great many things, beginning with "Get the hell out of here."

"Stop it!" I said sharply. "I want to make a deal with you."

His eyes narrowed. "What kind of a deal?"

"I won't tell the police about that package, if you tell me what you saw last night, when Scotty was killed."

He licked his lips. "What makes you think I saw anything?"

"You saw enough to know you'd never have to answer to Scotty no matter what outrageous lies you told us about him. You knew you could say anything you felt like and he'd never hear about it and he'd never lay a finger on you. Never! Because he was dead! At least, you *thought* he was dead."

"You're trying to frame me for his murder," he said sullenly.

"I couldn't frame you even if I wanted to. Because of the gun. The person who shot Scotty stole the gun from somebody out here—and you didn't even know that gun existed. You were off the island at the only time you could have learned about it. Do you understand?"

He nodded.

"The police know you didn't shoot Scotty, and I know it. All I want you to do is to help me find the killer."

His eyes narrowed again. "Why? What's in it for you?"

"The police are off on the wrong trail. They're questioning the wrong person, a friend of mine."

"Oh." He leered at me. "The boyfriend's in trouble."

I winced and looked away.

He propped himself up on his elbow again. "If I tell you what I saw, how do I know you'll keep your part of the bargain?"

"You don't. You'll just have to take my word for it."

He thought about that a minute. "I want to sit up straighter. Help me." He leaned forward.

I raised the back of the lounge and secured it.

"There's not much to tell," he said sullenly. "The ferry I was on sat out the storm in Kismet, so it was a half-hour late getting here. I went home for a bit and then I—"

"How long were you home?"

"Long enough to let the dog out and dump a can of food on his plate. Five minutes, maybe. I was restless, so I decided to go to Ocean Beach and look for a little excitement. It had stopped raining, and I thought I'd walk there, on the beach. When I got to the beach, it was

175

so foggy I couldn't see a thing; I was even afraid I'd run into the lifeguard stand! Just as I reached the bottom of the stairs, I heard a gun go off. Only I didn't know it was a gun at the time. Even though that one particular bang sounded different, I still thought it was the ocean, which was banging and booming so loud you couldn't hear yourself think. Anyway, I went down to the edge of the water where the sand was hard enough to walk on, and I almost stepped on him! Jesus! He was lying there, face down, in a couple of inches of water. The tide was coming in, and each time a wave hit the shore, it jiggled him a little."

"Did you see who shot him?"

He licked his lips. "I saw somebody, just for an instant, off ahead in the fog. I just caught a glimpse of his back."

"Was he tall or short?" I asked carefully. John Wohlens was six-feet-four.

"I couldn't tell. I saw him just for a second, and then he was gone in the fog." He licked his lips again. "I told you it wasn't much."

"What did you do then?"

"I got the hell out of there. It was starting to rain again, and I changed my mind about walking to Ocean Beach. I decided to ride over, if I could catch the lateral ferry, and if I couldn't, I was going to go home. I figured that the lateral would be half an hour late, like the rest of the ferries. I hit it lucky; it was ready to pull away from the dock when I got down to Center, but it waited for me."

"One more thing," I said. "When you saw Scotty lying there, did you check to see if he was still alive?"

Carl shook his head.

"Did you call the police?"

"No."

"Or tell anyone that there was a wounded man lying at the edge of the water?"

"No. I didn't want to get involved." He took out a pack of cigarettes from the breast pocket of his shirt and lit up.

"You could have called them from a pay phone in Ocean Beach and not given your name. You might have saved his life. Did you think of that?"

"No. Why should I? It wasn't any of my business." He smoked in silence for a moment. "Do you think you know who killed him?"

I nodded.

"If you want me to," he said slowly, "maybe I could add a few particulars for the police—like he was tall, or thin, or dark-haired—whatever you want me to say."

What a terrible man! I thought.

"Just tell the truth, and I'll keep my end of the bargain."

24

IT WAS A quarter past four when I crossed the walk and opened the garbage can in the shed by the foot of the Wohlens' ramp——not the empty can that Paula had put away, but its companion, which should have been empty, too. Only it wasn't. After the early morning pickup, somebody had put it back in the shed and placed some garbage inside—in a white plastic bag, the size that fits in a kitchen can.

From his redwood bench on the Ballou's side deck, Carl was watching me. I didn't care. I unwound the metal tie around the neck of the bag and picked through the contents as carefully as a shopping bag lady searching for a meal.

What I found inside was a dinner for two—not the remains, but the complete meal, scooped up and thrown out before anyone had eaten a bite: a flank steak, cooked but not sliced; two potatoes, baked but never opened; a small, round chocolate cake; and lots of limp, lifeless lettuce in its dressing, smelling of garlic, clinging to everything else. It was Paula and John's dinner; I knew, because the chocolate cake was still in its box from William Greenberg, Jr. Desserts.

What happened? Why hadn't they eaten? And why did John hang around Sharon's Landing long enough to take out the garbage after the Sunday morning pickup?

I closed the garbage can, hurried up the ramp, let myself in through the bathroom door, and began to search the house.

I started with the master bedroom. A puffy down comforter served as a spread for the big double bed. The jeans Paula had taken off lay on top—one leg inside out—next to her white shirt, navy poncho, and a briefcase, which I opened; there was nothing inside except the financial section of the Sunday *Times*. The clothes in the closet were all hers—two sets of warmups, a frayed terry robe, a nightgown, slightly soiled, the white slacks and striped cotton sweaters she wore to parties, the tan pants she gardened in, two hooded sweatshirts, two tennis hats on the top shelf, and on the bottom, torn sneakers (for clamming?), low-heeled white sandals, and Top-Siders, with dirty socks stuffed in the toes. I rifled through the underwear, nightgowns, and bathing suits in the bureau, and checked the night tables. The one on the left side of the bed held hand cream, emery boards, a sewing kit; in the one on the right, I found a flashlight and a bottle of aspirin.

I checked my watch. It was twenty-five to five already, and what had I found? Nothing.

I hurried into John's study and opened his desk. I found a stack of instruction booklets for the kitchen equipment, some charge receipts from Frank's grocery, and a pile of summer ferry schedules—one for each community on the island—which cheered me a lot. While they wouldn't prove anything to Harry, not by themselves, anyway, I knew that John needed those schedules in order to arrive at the ferry dock in Ocean Beach or Cherry Grove at exactly the right minute; if he had to race to catch the boat, or if he had to wait around too long for it to leave, somebody might notice him and remember him.

There was a bed in the study, a single bed. It was missing its spread—a red one, if I remembered right, of heavy cotton cord. Where was it? In the laundry? I checked the hamper in the guest bathroom, which had nothing in it, and the washer and dryer out on the back deck. The washer was stuffed with damp, sour-smelling beach towels, and the dryer was empty.

When I came back in the study, I noticed John's brown loafers at the foot of the bed, side by side, the toes pointing toward the closet door, which was half open. I opened it the rest of the way and looked in the closet at John's Fire Island clothes—his blue and tan warmup suit, a pair of jeans, some chinos, a heavy wool pullover, a poncho, a tan windbreaker—and a faded blue work shirt hanging on a hook behind the windbreaker. The pocket of the work shirt had something in it. I unbuttoned the flap, pulled out a red plastic property owner's tag, and stared at it numbly, not believing what I saw. Then I heard someone walk on the deck. I dove into the closet, crawled over two pairs of sneakers, and sat down on a pile of clothes.

Go away, I prayed, whoever you are.

Whoever it was tried the front door, found it was locked, and knocked sharply. "Anyone there?" a male voice called.

For an instant, I thought it was John, and then he said, "Lily! Are you in there?" and I knew it was Harry. Carl must have told him where I was. Limp with relief, I started to crawl out of the closet. Then I stopped and sat down again. How could I face Harry? What could I say? That I had a perfect case against John Wohlens until thirty seconds ago when I discovered the tag—the evidence that he hadn't killed Scotty.

"Lily!" he called, "are you in there?"

I sat perfectly still, waiting for him to decide I'd been here and gone, listening to his exasperated sigh, and, finally, to the sound of his footsteps going down the ramp. I'll give him three minutes, I thought, and began to count the seconds. When I reached one-hundred eighty, I leaned back against the closet wall and took a deep breath. The smell of tobacco smoke caught in the clothes overhead mingled with the damp odors from the sneakers—and with something else. A pleasant, familiar smell. Chocolate.

I stood up and pushed aside the hangers and found the light switch. Then I picked up the clothes I'd been sitting on piece by piece—John's brown tweed jacket with the suede elbow patches, brown slacks, brown knit tie, white shirt, brown socks, white undershirt, and light blue boxer shorts. Under them all, lying on top of his new tennis racquet, was a cardboard box, with the Brooks Brothers logo in the center, squashed and broken from being sat on. It could have held a tennis shirt, or some brand new jockey shorts, or half a dozen pairs of tennis socks, but it didn't. It was lined with aluminum foil and filled with chocolate brownies.

If I'd been a little less proud and a lot more prudent, I would have walked into the kitchen that moment and called Harry. And I did plan to call him, of course—as soon as I figured out what had happened here last night before Scotty arrived with his chocolate brownies. All I needed was a few more minutes. There's time, I told myself. Paula won't be back for a quarter of an hour—or maybe longer, if the four of them stand around and talk after they finish playing.

I spread out the clothes on top of the bed, placed the box of brownies and the tennis racquet beside them, and asked myself why everything ended up on the closet floor. To hide the brownies? Not likely. There were better places and better ways to conceal them than under a pile of clothes—good clothes that belonged on hangers, clothes that John should have worn back to the city. He probably planned to wear them. He took his loafers out of the closet, and he must have taken out the rest of his clothes at the same time. Laid them on the bed. Just before he showered, perhaps, or while he was waiting for

Paula to fix dinner. Only they never ate the dinner. Something happened. Something terrible.

I shivered and looked at the clothes again, lying on the bed just the way they must have been last evening. Except for one thing; one thing, I figured, was different. When John took out the clothes he planned to wear and the tennis racquet he planned to take with him, and when Scotty came by after the storm and left his box of brownies behind, the red cord spread was on the bed. Someone, someone who needed the spread, scooped up all the things on top of it and dumped them into the closet.

Needed the spread for what?

I left the study and came into the kitchen and made myself a gin and tonic. Then I carried it over to the sliding-glass doors in the living room and tried to puzzle out what someone did with a red cord bedspread. By the time I finished my drink, I thought I knew the answer. But it was five past five already, and Paula was hurrying up the walk from the tennis courts.

She climbed the ramp, and when she stepped on the deck, I opened the door.

She gasped and dropped her racquet. "Lily!" She stooped to pick it up without taking her eyes off me. "How did you get in?"

"The back door was unlocked." I moved aside to let her pass, feeling uncertain and cowardly as I watched her drop her hat and dark glasses on the kitchen table, prop her racquet against the side of the bar, and place her tote bag on the kitchen counter in the corner by the refrigerator.

"How was your game?" I asked, as though no one had died and nothing had changed.

"Terrible." She tore a paper towel off the roll over the sink and wiped her forehead. "Just terrible."

Her face was flushed; perspiration stained her white

shirt under the arms and soaked her hair, shaping it flat against her head. She rubbed her eyes hard with her finger tips, and when she took her hands away, I saw that her eyelids were swollen and covered with a pink rash. She had poison ivy.

"I need a drink." She dropped an ice cube into a water glass, poured enough Scotch on top of it for three drinks, and took a deep swallow.

"Where's John?" I asked.

"In Philadelphia. I told you." She sipped the Scotch, watching me carefully over the rim of the glass.

"Call him."

"I can't. I don't know where he is. I'll call him at the college at the end of the week, if you tell me what this is all about."

"Why didn't he take his tennis racquet when he left the island?"

"Didn't he?" Her eyes narrowed. "I suppose he didn't need it. He said something about being too busy to play for a while." She tilted the glass and drank deeply.

"That's a lie!" I said, hearing my voice rise. "He was supposed to play in a tournament next week. He told me so, coming over on the ferry. And why didn't he take his tweed jacket and his tie and the rest of the clothes he wore coming out here? Why were they all dumped on the closet floor?"

"What are you up to?" she snapped. "We're supposed to be good friends. And then you sneak in here and poke around and—"

"Find what I didn't want to find," I said heavily. "That John's dead. That you killed him."

She studied me for a moment. "Come over here, Lily," she said gently.

She pulled out a chair for me at the kitchen table, and I sat down.

"Give me your drink and I'll freshen it."

"No." I covered my glass with my hand.

She shrugged and perched herself on the tall kitchen stool and placed her drink on the bar. "I know what's the matter, Lily. We all know—your children, your friends, everybody. The psychiatrist you told me about said you were deeply depressed over losing Henry. Depression warps people; they can't see things clearly; sometimes they even imagine things that don't exist."

"I'm not imagining anything! You killed John. Then you killed Scotty."

"You think I killed Scotty, too?" She shook her head sadly. "You're not yourself, Lily. Try to understand that."

"Scotty was here," I went on doggedly, "in this house. Right before he was shot. I know it because he was carrying some brownies, and I found the brownies in the bottom of John's closet. They were packed in a box from Brooks Brothers."

She remembered the box. She stiffened and gulped down the last of the Scotch. "You're talking nonsense. I couldn't have shot Scotty; I wasn't here. Just now, down at the courts, Taki said that Scotty was shot at a quarter to ten. I left Fire Island on the eight-twenty-five ferry, and there was no way, in that storm, that I could have gotten back here in time! Ask Al Fry. He saw me catching the ferry. Or Frank from the store. He saw me boarding."

"Frank told me. But he also said that he left the dock and went back to the store before the ferry pulled out—in plenty of time for you to change your mind and get off again. In that crowd, nobody who didn't know you would have noticed."

"Prove it!" she said harshly. "You can't prove a thing. Nobody's going to believe your crazy stories." She placed her glass on the bar and pushed it away. "Go ahead and tell your detective friend that I killed my husband. He'll think you're a loony. Where's the body, he'll say."

I stood up and walked to the front of the bar. "You buried the body, Paula. Wrapped it in the red bedspread from John's study and dragged it out of the house and down the ramp. I don't know for sure where you buried it, but I'll suggest to Lieutenant Bell that his men start digging right by the pile of boards under Elmo Kesselbaum's new deck."

She gasped, and her face turned ashen. She gulped the rest of her Scotch, put the glass on the bar, and then shoved it away from her. It skidded in my direction, and I caught it before it went over the edge. I felt sick. My stomach churned, fighting the gin.

"Why did you do it? Why? Why did you kill him? Tell me," I pleaded. "You're my friend. I have to know!"

Her lips formed a smile. "Why do you think?"

"He must have threatened you. Or attacked you." I caught my breath. "You wouldn't have—"

"Oh, wouldn't I?" She slid off the stool and paced to the refrigerator and back to the table, her eyes on the terra cotta tiles on the floor. Then she stopped and raised her head. "He was going to leave me," she said softly. "He was going to leave me for some empty-headed woman he met at the Lynfield tennis club!" Her mouth turned down in distaste. "Yesterday afternoon, when it was so hot and we all left the court before we were supposed to, I overheard him talking to her on the phone—plotting with her. He didn't know I had heard anything until right before dinner. He opened the wine and was pouring a glass for me when I told him. Straight out. That's usually the best way to handle things with John. I thought he'd be upset and grovel a little, and promise never to see her again. But no."

Paula stood rigid, staring past me, out the sliding-glass doors. "He said he was in love with her and wanted to marry her, and that he planned to ask me for a divorce as soon as he signed the job contract with the college. He hoped I'd understand, he said, smiling that crooked smile he always used on me when he wanted something special. Money, usually." She shuddered. "The nerve of the man! I felt like spitting on him. I picked up my wine glass and threw the wine in his face. He wiped it off very calmly with the napkins on the table and said he didn't have to put up with me anymore; he had a good job where people respected him and a sweet, beautiful wife-to-be who would bring him happiness. Then he went in his study and slammed the door and locked it.

"I was so enraged I could hardly breathe. I didn't know what to do, and then I remembered that big, black gun Caroline had out on her deck when we came off the court, and I decided to go get it and frighten him with it—show him I meant business. Will and Caroline were gone; I saw Will leave, and then Caroline went out a little later. I walked in their house and into the bedroom and found the gun easy as pie. It was empty but I found the bullets and loaded it."

"Oh, no," I breathed.

"I brought it back here, and then I knocked on the study door and said, 'Please let me come in.' After a minute, he opened the door. He'd laid out all his city clothes on the bed—he was still in his tennis things, all stained with wine—and he'd started packing his duffle suitcase.

" 'You're not going to leave me,' I told him and pointed the gun at his heart. He kept packing. 'Oh, yes I am.' I released the safety. He heard the sound and started, but he thought I was just trying to frighten him; he didn't dream I'd pull the trigger. And maybe I wouldn't have, if he'd looked a little frightened, or a little less determined, or if only he'd said something kind to me." She rubbed her eyes. "But he didn't. He just raised his head and looked at me with such hatred and scorn that I knew it was the end. Jesus! I felt like I was being buried alive. 'You won't abandon me!' I shouted. 'I won't let you.' And pulled the trigger. He fell over backwards, and he was dead before he hit the floor. I panicked, Lily. I was sure the whole community heard the shot—even though the ocean was crashing and booming—and all I could think about was getting away, as fast as I could. It was five after eight; I could still make the eight-twenty-five ferry if I rode down to Fair Harbor on my trike.

"I grabbed a poncho, stuffed my purse in a tote, and pedaled down as fast as I could. The main dock was jammed with young people, talking and drinking and eyeing each other. I was about to push through the crowd when Al Fry came out of the liquor store and said 'Oh, you're leaving,' and asked where John was. I said he was loading our things on the ferry. I was surprised at how calm I was, how normal I acted.

"As I boarded, I waved at Frank from the store, who was seeing a group of people off. And as I sat down next to a window, I noticed that Frank was walking back to the store, and that Al was gone. At that moment, I stopped running and started using my brain. The ferry captain had started the engine, but passengers were still boarding. With my poncho on and the hood pulled up, I stepped off the ferry and joined the crowd seeing them off. As the ferry pulled out, and everyone on shore watched it and waved at their friends, I walked around to the left of the freight house, crossed Bay, hiked up Elm to Center Walk, and down to the ocean on Oak. There were only a few people on the walks, and none of them even looked at me.

"Nobody was on the beach all the way through Dune-wood and Sharon's Landing—it was raining by then. I came off in Lonelyville and walked through the reeds and brush into my back yard. The storm hit just as I reached my house, and the lights went out. I lit a candle and carried it into John's study and forced myself to look at his body. While the thunder crashed and the lightning crackled and flashed, I stared at him, studied him.

"The longer I looked, the calmer I felt. I was glad I shot him. I wondered how I ever could have loved him. I hated him, now—for his inability to hold a job, his vanity, his childish self-importance—and his foolish attempt to leave me. I was glad he was dead and I was alive, and I vowed I'd stay alive. While the storm raged on, I decided on a plan to save myself. It took a long time to carry out; I had to wait until the middle of the night to bury the body—and then I cleaned the house and showered and dressed, and caught the first ferry in the morning out of Ocean Beach. Nobody noticed me." She smiled for the first time. "There were maybe twenty people boarding; at least ten of us were wearing blue ponchos."

She pushed her bangs away and rubbed her eyes again.

She hasn't slept at all, I thought. How could she ever sleep again? For an instant, pity stirred me.

"I'm sorry about Scotty; I really am." She brought her tote bag to the bar and climbed up on the kitchen stool again. "But he came to the house at just the wrong time to talk to me about some problem he had. I was in the bathroom with the water running and didn't hear him knock or call or whatever he did. But he saw a light in the back of the house—I left the candle burning in John's study—and he came in anyway; he thought I might be in trouble. I found him bending over John's body." She shook her head sadly. "I had to get rid of him. You understand?"

"No, I don't. Paula, how could you—"

But she ignored me. "Know how I got him out of the house and down to the ocean? I told him I was going to

188

drown myself. Only I let him think he might be able to talk me out of it. All the way down to the edge of the water I listened to him spout nonsense—how I should give myself up and plead temporary insanity."

"He was right, you know," I said gently, still thinking I could help her, reason with her. "If you—"

"I'm not going to plead anything! You want me to ruin my life? There isn't a mayor or senator in the whole country who'd ever ask my advice again if he knew about this!"

I was frightened now, for the first time, though I didn't see how she could hurt me. The police had Caroline's gun. If she made a move to open the drawer by the sink where she kept her kitchen knives, I'd run out the front door. But I knew I'd made a mistake not calling Harry when I had the chance—and then I made another mistake and glanced at the phone on the wall by the bar.

She saw me and nodded. "And now you want to tell your detective friend you've found his killer. All by yourself." She grinned slyly. "He doesn't know what's under Elmo's deck, does he? Only you and I know."

She reached in her tote, took out a small, gray gun, and pointed it at me.

"Don't be a fool, Paula!" I was in a panic and tried not to show it. "I've been talking to people about you and John; they'll tell Lieutenant Bell even if I can't. He'll come over here and find the same evidence I found."

"I'll destroy it," she said calmly. "I'll go through every inch of this house and the only traces I'll leave will all point to John. When your Lieutenant Bell finds them, I'll be forced to tell him that John didn't leave with me on the *Fair Harbor ferry*; that he stayed to keep an appointment with Scotty; and that I waited in the car in Bay Shore until he arrived on the last ferry from Ocean Beach. I'll say I didn't know he shot Scotty; I'll say I drove him to Penn Station this morning at nine; when he doesn't turn up at Lynfield next Tuesday, they'll think he's skipped. It all fits, you see. All I have to do is get rid of you." She waved the gun at me.

"Listen, Paula," I said desperately. "I'm your friend. I'll always be your friend. I'll never desert you, no matter what happens. Don't add my death to the others; you won't be able to bear it!"

She shifted the gun around in her hand. "Pretty little thing, isn't it? I bought it when John took the job in Lynfield. I felt safer; our apartment in New York isn't as protected as yours is. I'm a good shot, Lily." She walked over to me and touched my cheek with the gun barrel.

I gasped and began to quake. "Don't shoot," I blubbered. "Please don't shoot me!"

She drew back, smiling. "Maybe I won't have to. I'm going to give you a choice. A bullet in the head—through the mouth, I think; it would keep you from talking even if it didn't kill you right away. Or a nice, gentle, easy way out with a bottle full of sleeping pills. No pain, no bother, no blood." She fumbled around in a drawer in the bar and placed a bottle of pills on the dining table in front of me. "Halcion. We use the same brand. I'm doing this for you because you're my friend. Either way, of course, I'll fix it to look like suicide. Poor Lily!" She shook her head in mock pity. "So depressed about the death of her husband, unable to go on living without him! Her friends and her psychiatrist should have expected it."

"Give me a minute to think. Oh, please!" I pleaded. "Just a minute."

She nodded and backed herself up on the bar stool.

I closed my eyes and prayed *please God let me live* and tried to think, over the panic and the nausea.

"Well?"

I opened my eyes and saw her motion with the gun.

My lips moved, and I heard myself say, "The pills."

"Open them."

I tried to lift the cap, but my hands were shaking so much, I couldn't budge it. I put it in my mouth and tried to open it with my teeth, but nothing happened.

"Line up the tab on the lid with the slot. Hurry." Her mouth turned down in an ugly frown.

I managed to do what she said and pushed at the tab, which flew off so suddenly that I dropped the container, which fell on the floor.

"Oh," I breathed. "I'm sorry. I'll get it." And leaned down and with a mighty effort, grabbed a leg of the stool and swung it up into the air.

She fired as she went over backwards. I felt the bullet whiz past my shoulder, and I heard her head bang on the floor, and the gun bounce against the stove. I picked it up and pointed it at her, but she was limp and motionless. For a moment, I thought I'd killed her, but then I saw her chest rise and fall gently. I took the phone off the hook and called my house. Harry Bell answered.

25

HALF AN HOUR later, there were more policemen in Sharon's Landing than tennis players. They carried their cameras and equipment into the Wohlens' house and then out again across the walk, trampling on the poison ivy around the pile of old boards under Elmo's new back deck. When they began removing the boards, I left. Weaving my way around the squad cars blocking Ocean Walk, I went home. Sergeant Brady, on the phone at the card table, waved. Mops thumped his tail and whined to go out.

"Later," I said and fixed myself a tall, clinky Perrier and lime and took it out on the deck. The water was choppy; tin-can–silver waves and triangular black shadows, like the snouts of sharks, bounced around on the restless ocean. I sipped my drink and brooded.

Not about Paula. She had tried to kill me and I was still too agitated about that to give her a minute's pity or concern. It was Caroline who had bothered me, rattled my conscience, loaded me up with guilt—right from the beginning, when we boarded the ferry at the Bay Shore terminal. I should have paid attention. I've been fooling myself, I thought. I'm not the kind of woman who could steal somebody else's husband. Even if he allowed himself to be stolen!

I wove back through the squad cars to look for Will. I'd seen him fifteen minutes ago on the walk, talking to Harry Bell. But Harry was gone—on the helicopter, back to the mainland, Fred Mulloy said, and Fred hadn't seen Will since I had.

They were just removing the body—a tarpaulin-covered heap strapped on a stretcher. Four men carried it down to the ferry dock and maneuvered it onto a police launch bouncing on the waves. Most of my neighbors watched the procession, huddled in somber groups along the route or on the Rosens' deck down at the bay.

Will wasn't anywhere around, and Caroline, at the Rosen's, didn't know where he'd gone.

I went home for my bike and looked for him every place I could think of—the oceanfront, the grocery aisles, the general store, the liquor store, even the postage-stamp bar in the back of the restaurant. I gave up, finally, and took myself for a long, mindless ride, pedaling all the way to the western end of Saltaire, and then zigzagging up to the bay and back on each of the wide, beautiful, diagonally slatted wooden walks. For almost an hour, I didn't have a single thought about husbands and wives or crime and punishment.

When I biked back to Sharon's Landing, the squad cars had vanished and all the policemen, except for a lonesome pair patrolling in front of the Wohlens' house. Even Sergeant Brady had abandoned his post in my living room, taking away his phones and washing out all my coffee cups and clamshell ashtrays. Only Mops greeted me when I walked in. There were two notes on the oak table: one, from the Jessups, canceling their party; the other, from Harry, was so brief it almost didn't count: "I'll be in touch," it began. "H. B.," it ended. Nothing in between.

IV
Monday, July 4

26

I SLEPT AROUND the clock—from ten at night to ten in the morning—and I might have slept longer if the dog hadn't needed a walk.

It was drizzling and dark outside. On the way back to my house, I stopped at the top of the beach stairs and looked out at the rough, gray ocean. A heavy surf boomed down the beach and cut a deep ledge in the sand at the shoreline.

Inside, while I waited for the coffee to brew, I made a batch of ginger cookies and put them in the oven. When they were lacy around the edges, I took them out.

Caroline Mortimer rapped on the glass door to the kitchen; I motioned for her to come in.

"Ginger cookies," she said. "Oh, my. The whole place smells delicious."

"I'll give you a sample as soon as they cool. How about some coffee, Caroline?"

"Yes, please." She sat down at my oak table. "I still can't believe that Paula . . . "

"I don't want to talk about it," I said roughly. "Next month, maybe. Or next year."

"I'm sorry. I was just making conversation." She looked into the steaming mug I set in front of her. "I really came to thank you for bringing me home Saturday night. And for being straight with me about Millie." She ran a bright red fingernail over the scars on the table, took a deep breath, and finally stopped avoiding what she came to ask me. "Lily, do I need to go to AA or see a psychiatrist about my drinking?"

I took a cautious sip of coffee. "It seems to me that you do. You haven't been drinking heavily for very long, and you drink a lot less than you own up to. So it might be possible to switch to Perrier on your own. But why take a chance when you have so much at stake? Think about how Millie would feel if she knew you drank. And think about Will." I hunted around in my utilities drawer for the spatula. "He worries himself silly over your binges—for the moment—but one of these days, he'll stop worrying. And then he'll leave you, sure as anything. If I were you, I'd play it safe and get some help."

I brought a plate of cookies to the table.

She ate three and drank a little coffee. "Thank you." She looked at her watch. "I have to go now."

The sun made its appearance late in the day, just in time to set. I showered and dressed, for the trip back to the city, in jeans and my conch belt and a new, pale blue shirt. Then I sat on the deck for a while, watching the sunset stain the sand pink and the ocean lavender. The beach was deserted except for a single fisherman, hip-deep in glittering surf, casting his line, reeling in slowly, and patiently casting again. I counted ten casts and went inside.

It was still too early to leave for the ferry, but I was restless, and Mops scratched at the kitchen door and whined to go out.

I hooked on his leash, picked up my tote bag, and led him down the ramp to the first pine tree in the Milgrim yard. A man and a woman jogged slowly around the corner from Holly. I moved off the walk to let them pass, and so did Will, coming up from Blueberry. He was barefoot, wearing tennis clothes—his white shirt and shorts caught the fading light.

He still had time to bathe and dress and make the ferry if he said hello and goodbye and raced on home. But he didn't. He followed me to Holly and watched the dog sniff the remains of Matilda Huff's day lilies; the deer had eaten off their tops.

"Caroline says you were looking for me last evening."

I nodded. "Where were you hiding?"

"In one of the phone booths next to the grocery store."

"Oh. I never thought to look there." We moved on to the juniper bushes in front of the Van Burens' neat cedar house. Everything was cedar—even the garbage shed.

Will placed his hand on the shed roof. "I was talking to Millie. For almost an hour. Lieutenant Bell found her number in one of her letters to Scotty and gave it to me."

"He's a nice man," I offered.

"She cried a lot about Scotty; but she talked a lot too. Told me where she'd worked and where she'd lived after she left us—and the problems she had at home. She cried again—about us—and then she asked me to fly out to Los Angeles and bring her back! I'm going there Friday."

"You must be walking on air."

"I am," he said heavily. "I am."

"Then what's the matter?"

"I really stopped by to tell you I won't be taking the ferry and going into the city with you tonight, the way we, ah . . ." He studied the yellow and black pansies in the flower bed next to the Van Burens' ramp. "I told Caroline I'd stay over and take the red-eye out of Ocean Beach tomorrow morning. She and I have a lot of things to talk over before I can bring Millie home." He looked down at the pansies again. "I don't think we should see each other. Not for a while, anyway," he said stiffly.

"Buck up, Will. I'm uncomplicating things right now. And not just for a while. For good. It's better for you and Caroline. And it's much, much better for me," I added softly.

27

THE *ISLE OF FIRE* waited at the dock, pulling on her lines like a frisky horse. The entry door was shut, and none of the twenty-odd people waiting in the yellow haze of the dock light had boarded yet. But Harry Bell sat topside on the first bench behind the wheelhouse, his left arm resting on the side railing.

I was pleased to see him. Very pleased. I grinned at him, showing it. "Who gave you permission to board before anyone else?"

"The captain." He grinned back. "It's one of my perks. Well, actually, I never got off. I rode over with him from Bay Shore. To look for you, when you didn't turn up at the terminal on the ferry before this one."

"Bay Shore," the deckhand called, sliding open the entry door. "All aboard." He helped the nervous young couple lift their large baby carriage over the black slit of water between the dock and the ferry.

"Are you alone?" Harry asked.

I nodded.

"Give me your things."

I handed up my tote and the heavy Irish fisherman's sweater Henry and I bought in Dublin years ago.

The two Rosen families, their guests, and their children boarded next. Then Bo Jessup talking earnestly to Brian MacKay. Then a couple from Dunewood, and the woman with green toenails from Lonelyville, and a lot of other people I didn't know. Then it was my turn.

Harry gave me the seat by the side rail and petted the

dog, who wagged his tail politely, curled up on the deck between us, and went to sleep with his head on my foot.

The captain turned on the engines.

Toby Van Buren, in her mother's arms on the dock, called, " 'Bye, Daddy!"

Ernie Van Buren, three rows behind us, threw her kisses.

"All aboard!" the deckhand called. He slid the entry door in place, and came topside to pull his lines off the stanchions.

Sharon Jessup waved a last time to Bo, turned her red wagon around, and pulled it off the dock with its precious load: Matthew, Mark and Casey Jessup—bathed, pajamaed, sleepy-eyed. The ferry backed away from the dock and turned north, into the channel.

Harry said, "I talked to Al Fry at the hospital, a couple hours ago. Know what he was doing Saturday night when Mr. Zarrow saw him? Walking over to the Mortimers'! He couldn't bear to telephone Dr. Mortimer about his stomach pains, but he thought he could bring up the subject face to face. Crazy, isn't it, to be so terrified of doctors?"

The *Isle of Fire* raised its prow and bobbed over the wake of a power boat.

"He never made it to the Mortimers'; he felt so rotten he had to turn back and drag himself home to bed. He's fine, now, Mrs. Fry said for me to tell you, though the doctors say he's overweight and want him to go on a diet."

I slipped on my sweater and talked Harry into putting on the navy sweatshirt of Henry's I was carrying back to the city to be repaired.

Then I surprised myself by asking about Paula.

"I can't tell you much." Harry crossed his right leg over his left knee. "The doctor says she has a concussion, and he wants to keep her quiet for a few days before

201

we talk to her. And her lawyer's making very certain we follow his instructions! Her lawyer's Jo-Ellen MacKay. Rose house on Center Walk."

The ferry turned west, paralleling the two bay islands—black shapes silhouetted against the dove-gray sky. Across the inky water to the south, a ferry was loading at Fair Harbor, and lights shone in all the big bayfront houses in Saltaire.

"Funny thing," Harry went on, "you can never tell how a jury's going to rule on a woman who kills her unfaithful husband. They might have set her free if she hadn't killed Scotty as well."

"With a big assist from Carl Hayes," I offered.

He turned and stared at me. "Are you serious?"

"Of course I am! Oh, I know Paula shot Scotty and left him to drown. But Carl finished the job." I told him what Carl had told me about finding Scotty at the edge of the beach. "Carl assumed he was dead. But Scotty was alive then," I said. "He had to have been alive! Paula pulled the trigger only a minute or two earlier; Carl heard the shot. Moreover, Carl actually saw Paula, heading west up the beach toward Lonelyville—though from the back, and in the fog, he couldn't tell who it was, or even whether it was a man or a woman.

"And what do you think he did when he saw Scotty lying there? Pull him out of the water and turn him over to see if he was breathing? And then rush up the beach stairs and pound on the first door he came to with lights on and people inside, and tell them to get a doctor and the police? He walked away from him, that's what. Said it wasn't any of his business! He might have saved Scotty, but he didn't even try. I call that helping to murder him, don't you?"

He frowned and pulled on a sideburn. "It all depends on what the district attorney calls it. But even if we can't pin a charge on him, the narcs will. Fredericka Borg told us she saw Carl drop a packet into the poison ivy out his back window when his house was burning. With his broken ankle, he couldn't retrieve it, but we could. And when we told Mrs. Borg it held four ounces of cocaine, she said she wanted to testify against him. Her son died from an overdose."

We turned north at the buoy opposite Kismet into the open water of the bay. The last strands of the sunset had faded, and a bright star shone in the west. A ball of light, the first of the Fourth-of-July evening, shot into the sky above Bay Shore and burst into a waterfall of silver sparks. We leaned back and watched the fireworks in silence until the spotlight on the top of the wheelhouse arced across the Bay Shore bulkhead, and the captain cut the engine. The ferry rocked a little as it slowed and turned into the canal.

"Harry," I said, "I split with Will Mortimer. For good." Then I started to explain. "I'm not the kind of woman who—"

"No, you're not." He smiled. "How do you feel?"

I thought for a moment. "Relieved. Great, as a matter of fact. And hungry as a bear. I haven't eaten a thing since lunch."

"I'll buy you dinner," he said.

The ferry rolled into its slot at the terminal; the deck-hand lassoed the stanchions and secured his lines, and the captain turned off the engine and jumped down onto the dock.

We stood up, waiting our turn to leave.

"How about Chinese?" Harry asked.

If you have enjoyed this mystery and would like to
receive details of other Walker mysteries,
please write to:

Mystery Editor
Walker and Company
720 Fifth Avenue
New York, New York 10019